NIO

Mike Herd

Niobium © copyright Mike Herd

FIRST PAPERBACK EDITION 2023

Published by Scope Publishing
ISBN 978 1 7394728 1 8

The characters portrayed in this book are fictional and any similarity to people living in the real world is entirely coincidental.

Also by the Author

Niobium
Justice for Lydia
Sea Lavender
No Tears for Destiny
The Spirit of Askival
The Medusa Shield

NIOBIUM

In the early morning light, fog over the Jordan River was just beginning to clear. Faint outlines of Salt Lake City's skyline slowly emerged. Air bubbles from the DPS Dive Team disturbed the surface of the dark slow running water. Below, poor visibility was hampering attempts to fasten four hooks onto a vehicle resting on the river bed. Parked at a small slipway Detective Harriet Sullivan had the engine of her unmarked Crown Victoria running, the window closed and the heater full on. She yawned and glanced at the crane driver in his cab waiting patiently for a line to be attached. The outside temperature on the instrument panel showed 21°F. Listening to police chatter on the radio, she put her head back, closed her eyes and yawned again. She had come straight from a New Year's Eve party and was still feeling the effects of the alcohol. She took out her phone and touched Home Smart. It showed an image of the inside of her fridge.

A sensor listing groceries required had scoured the internet looking for the best price putting in an order that would be delivered to a box on her porch with a one way flap. She clicked on security and saw there were no alerts. She closed the cover and glanced out the window. She shouldn't be here she should be at home sleeping it off. The hangover she knew would come hadn't kicked in yet. She thought about saying no to the Sergeant when he called but that would never do. It began to snow. Swirling large flakes soon obscured her view. Harriet switched on the wind-shield wipers just as the crane started up and the wire tightened. She sighed, put on a pair of gloves and a woollen hat given to her as a Christmas present, picked up a flash-light, switched off the engine and reluctantly got out of the car. The two police divers surfaced, gave the thumbs up and clambered aboard a large inflatable boat aided by two colleagues. A patrolman walked over to Harriet.

"Happy new year Sullivan."

"Happy new year to you too Brodie let's hope it will be. I thought you'd moved to Provo."

"I did. They wanted me back, couldn't do without me," he said with a straight face. "Nah, turned it down, the wife wasn't too happy about the move."

Where is everybody?"

"Well there's just the three of us at the moment plus the divers the rest are on the way," he shrugged, "its New Year's Day."

"Well somebody had to draw the short straw. Who spotted the car?"

"It was the Polar Bear plunge group."

"The what?"

"Every New Year's day they go for a swim to raise money for charity. They're mostly in their late sixties it's a wonder they survive the cold."

"They swim in weather like this?"

"Yup. In any kinda weather, they called 911 at 7.09am."

"Is that them in the coach up there in the lay-by?"

"Yup."

"Have you got a statement?"

"Yup."

"When you get a chance tell them to go home and Brodie stay warm it's too cold to be standing around here."

The crane started creaking as it took the strain. A vanilla coloured VW slowly emerged cascading dirty grey water back into the river. The crane driver expertly swung the car round and dropped it carefully onto a waiting police transporter aided by its driver. Harriet switched on the flash-light and peered inside. A man still wearing a seat belt was slumped forward onto the steering wheel and as the water drained she could see he had both hands clasped together. Harriet tried the doors and the trunk but it was locked. She looked along the slipway and noted there were no tracks and none on the river bank apart from her own, Officer Brodie's, DPS vehicle, the transporter and the crane.

"What do you think happened Sully?"

"I'm calling it a sudden death for now. Forensics will tell us more, until then I'm keeping an open mind. It could be just another suicide. Strange how it ended up in the river though."

She walked round it while putting a call through to the Division of Motor Vehicles. "How does a vehicle move forward into the river without leaving tracks?" she said to herself. "Hello this is Detective Sullivan I'd like the name and address of the owner of a VW license In God We Trust license plate number 8371C."

Sullivan wrote the name Joseph Simmons and his address and closed her notebook. She peered into the car again and took several photographs with her phone.

"You're a bit of puzzle Mr Simmons," she said, as she watched the trailer being towed away. She shivered and hurried over to her car, glad to get in and start the engine. It could be a stretch calling it her first murder investigation, there might be a simple explanation after all. She opened the laptop that was on the passenger seat and after inserting her password starting writing a preliminary report on what she knew so far, the colour and model of the car, its licence plate number, the time of the call in and by whom. She added her arrival time and transferred the images from her phone. Then out of the blue, without any warning she thought of Mitch. Her on, off boyfriend. She had all but given up on him and now he was distracting her.

"Focus," she said.

She wondered what he was doing at that very moment, probably somewhere hot.

"Stop it," she said out loud. "Where is this coming from?"

She finished her report after adding a few more details then saved it. She emailed it to an address held by her work PC.

"Bound to have a girl in every port," she said to herself.

Checking Simmons address, she put the car into drive and headed back to Salt Lake City.

Officer Joan Hardy had arrived early. She sat in the car with the engine running and the heater on full. She didn't know why she was here, but that was how things worked at her level in the police force. Need to know only and all she needed to know was this address to meet a detective. She looked over at the old red and terracotta brick Pair House with its simple four pane sash windows. It was clearly in need of attention showing settlement cracks that had been badly repaired signalling an air of neglect. A mature coniferous tree growing a little too close obscured a third of the house. There was no fence, no gate just a cement path with overly long grass on either side. She heard a car approach and looked in the mirror.

Harriet pulled in behind the patrol car as Officer Hardy got out. She noticed the curtains move and a face peering out. It was an anxious deathly pale face full of dread that Harriot had seen before. She looked at Hardy and nodded towards the door.

"Next of kin I'm afraid. I hate this part of the job. Come on, let's get this over with." They walked up the path and by the time they reached the door it had opened. "Mrs Melissa Simmons?" The woman nodded.

She was dark under her tired slate blue eyes. Wrinkles radiated from them deepening as she frowned. "It's about Joe isn't it?" She pushed back wisps of greying hair from her face that showed no sign of make-up or lipstick and put her hand to her mouth. She had clearly not slept at all.

"I'm Detective Sullivan and this is my colleague Officer Hardy can we come in?" She nodded and they entered. "Do you mind if I call you Melissa?" She shook her head. Harriet sat down while Hardy stood. "I'm Harriet. You posted your husband missing last night."

"Wait," she said patting her chest. "I suffer from asthma." She found an inhaler in her bag and breathed in an exact dose of steroid.

"I'm afraid I have some very bad news Melissa. Subject to a positive identification, your husband was recovered from the Jordan River still in his vehicle."

Mrs Simmons went white and closed her eyes. She stood up and left the room. They could hear sobbing next door. Hardy looked at Harriet who shook her head. Mrs Simmons came back in again carrying a handkerchief, blew her nose and sat down.

"Sorry about that."

"I have to ask you some questions if that's Ok. When was the last time you saw your husband?"

"It was after dinner I think about nine-thirty. We had run out of tonic…we both drink gin so he left for the store." She blew her nose again and wiped away the tears.

"Which store is it and how long would it take him to get there?"

"It's the 24Seven on Carpenter Avenue and it would have taken him, depending on the traffic about twenty minutes."

"Does he have a computer?"

"Yes he has a laptop, it's in the office."

"Is it alright if we take it away for examination?" she nodded, "he didn't have a cell phone with him what was his number?"

"That's strange. He always had his phone he wouldn't go anywhere without it and his tablet." She wrote his number on a piece of paper.

"Was he on medication, did he have any health issues?" Melissa shook her head, "what did he work at?"

"He was a freelance investigative journalist, a very good one."

"Do you know what he was working on?"

"He never discussed his work with me, said it was for the best. But…he must have been working on something big. He was very excited, tried to hide it but I could tell. I knew him better than he knew himself. I also recognised other things, like when he was working on something really important he would be totally focussed on it. Last night I had to remind him on his way out he was still wearing slippers."

"Did he take or make a call last night?"

"No but he did receive a couple of texts."

"Did he reply to them?"

"Yes he always replied to texts. I was so looking forward to welcoming in the New Year with him," she started crying.

"Do you have any family or friends nearby?"

"I have a sister in Montana but she's much older than me and can't get about much."

"Well Joan will stay with you for as long as you need and make sure you're alright, if there's anything you want just ask. I know this is not going to be easy but a formal identification is necessary. Whenever you feel strong enough but just take your time."

"Do you have any idea what happened to Joe, I mean, I don't understand how he came to be in the river…"

"I'm afraid not, it's too early. We need to do a lot of tests to find out how he died. If it's any comfort there was no sign of any physical injury. How his car ended up in the water is a mystery but I promise you Melissa we'll find out."

2

"Sullivan isn't it? What are you doing here? I thought you were attached to Vice."

Senior forensic pathologist Dr Henry Speed was measuring a knife wound in the chest of a black woman. An overhead fluorescent tube flickered on a panel of strip lights reflecting off his bald head. It was the only source of illumination in the uniformly pale green windowless morgue. Speed was fifty-eight years old and had spent the last twelve as Medical Examiner. People tended to avoid him partly because of his gruffness. He was never going to be the life and soul of any party but also because of the nature of his work. The only time he dabbled with the idea of hospitality was five years back when his wife was still alive. He accidentally invited some colleagues for a meal. They came simply because it was such an unusual invitation and they were curious about his home life. Half way through the meal he became so bored with the company that he described in graphic detail the finer points about dissecting the various organs in the body much to the annoyance of his wife. Just above Speed on the wall a sign read.

'This is the place where death rejoices to help those who live.'

"Happy New Year to you too," said Harriot. "I was in Vice now I'm in Homicide its Detective Sullivan by the way and this happens to be my first case."

He sighed. "Homicide eh? A very rare breed." He continued to delve into the open body. "There are only what six or seven

Detectives working in homicide?" He bowed slightly at the corpse. "My congratulations how did you manage to get the promotion? No matter, what is your first case?"

"Joseph Gideon Simmons, have you done the autopsy?"

Speed laughed, "Simmons? Someone's pulling your leg sending you on a wild goose chase on your first homicide. Why don't you run along and stop wasting my time I've got grown-up things to attend to. Raise a family, get your hair done, go shopping, do things normal women do."

Harriet sighed pretending to be injured. "Still living in the seventies Speed. Thankfully your kind is dying out just like all the other dinosaurs…well?"

Speed went to a steel sink and washed the blood off his gloves. "I have done a preliminary examination and, ex mea sententia (*in my opinion*) he died e causa ignota (*cause unknown*) possibly of natural causes, most likely a cardiac arrest. There was no water in his lungs therefore he died before his vehicle went into the river. Time of death is a little more difficult to estimate because of the low temperature of the water, however my best estimate is that he died between 10pm on New Year's Eve and 2am, can't be more specific than that. Now I have bodies stacked up in drawers here of genuine homicides waiting to be examined and I have to prioritize my time. I do not see the need for a full autopsy on Simmons. Experto crede." (*trust in the experienced*)

"I have spoken to his wife and she wishes her husband to be fully examined." Harriet crossed her fingers behind her back knowing he would have to comply.

"Damn it did you have anything to do with that? I am the senior Medical Examiner here and I decide whether there will be a full autopsy."

"You're on your own today," she said ignoring him, "isn't that against protocol?"

"It's New Year's day who in their right mind is going to come into a morgue when they could be out having fun."

"You...me," she said.

Dr Speed walked round a table with a dismembered woman's body and opened a drawer containing Simmons. He unzipped the body bag to reveal a face that looked strangely peaceful.

"Look I understand that this is probably your first alleged homicide and you want to prove something to Sergeant Stokes. You were given this because there's nothing in it. Stokes is being kind to you. I know how it goes; a new Detective is terrified of falling flat on her face on the first one. It's like standing at the edge of a precipice wondering if your parachute will open if you jump. Mark this closed. Nobody's going to remember your second case whatever the outcome."

Harriet gazed at him in silence, arms crossed. "Since when did you start worrying about the feelings of new Detectives?"

"Ok, what's this all about? What have you got?"

"Enough."

"Look I haven't got time to play games."

"It's at the very early stages but I believe there is enough circumstantial evidence to support further investigation. There are extenuating circumstances that don't stack up and since you clearly don't know anything about me, I'm not a great fan of coincidence."

"You'll have to get the Investigative Bureau Chief's green on this, my time's precious."

"Look the deceased wife wants a full autopsy, the IBC will want to know why he is being bothered under theses circumstance and if I was feeling uncharitable I would suggest to him that you were not just being unhelpful but obstructive. Live up to your name Henry I need it PDQ."

"Don't make an enemy of me Sullivan believe me it's not a good idea."

"Keep your hair on Henry," she said gazing at his shiny head, "there's nobody in the station going to know about this conversation. I need your co-operation. Tell you what if I nail this one you owe me if I don't, I owe you. Meanwhile can I have a copy of your preliminary?"

He shrugged his shoulders. "What do you have that I could possibly want?" Dr Speed was still washing his hands silently cursing. "Come through to the office," he said drying his hands.

They left the morgue walking along a corridor through swing doors turned right along another corridor and entered an open plan area with eight desks and computers. He sat down at the only one that was lit and typed in a password while Harriet stood waiting. A printer whirred and when it finished he handed the single A4 page to her. The barbed friendliness had gone and he was having to jump through hoops sulking.

"Is this it."

"I told you it was a preliminary examination."

"When will you be finished with Simmons?" she asked.

"When I'm finished."

"Let me just get this clear, when you examined him you found nothing?"

"That's correct."

"Nothing at all?"

"Nothing at all because there's nothing *to* find."

"If he died before his car went into the river how did it get there?" she asked.

Speed shrugged. "You're the detective, feci quod potui, faciant meliora potentes." *(I have done what I could let those who can, do better)*

Harriet pointed at him. "That's exactly what I intend to do."

Dr Speed looked at her in surprise.

Harriet left the morgue on N. Mario Capecchi Drive feeling it shouldn't have been that difficult to get him to do a full autopsy. She got into her car and opened the leather case taking out the report.

"AUTOPSY REPORT
18th February 2016
Autopsy UTH632864-43D
DECEASED: Joseph Gideon Simmons yet to be formally identified.
PRELIMINARY EXAMINATION by Dr Henry Speed.
Age: 49
Sex: Male
Race: White
Weight: 210 lbs.
Height: 65 inches
Hair: greying brown.
Eyes: blue
Clothing: Dark blue suit, White shirt, White underwear, Red tie, Black socks, Black shoes.
There are no signs of any external injuries.
No water in lungs
No signs of a cardiac arrest.
MRI scan shows no internal injuries.
Cause of death unknown.
Conclusion: Death by natural causes"

"What's the Latin for how long did that take you Dr Speed? Five minutes? I've never seen such a thin autopsy," she said to herself.

Harriet started the car and put the heater blower on full. She wiped the condensation from the wind shield with her gloved hand and while waiting for it to clear, drummed the steering wheel with her fingers. She wondered why that little interlude with Speed was so stressful? What was wrong with the guy? Maybe he was just a plain old fashioned misogynist she concluded. With the windows clearing she waited for a gap in the traffic, indicated then moved out heading south-east on 282. The temperature outside was still struggling to rise above freezing. The heater began to show signs of easing the chill inside the car. The traffic was slowing down. She stopped on the inside lane at the red lights of the junction of Foothill Drive. She pulled up he sun visor to see the light, waiting for it to change. She glanced in the mirror and switched on the radio. A large pale green Chevrolet Tahoe was approaching from behind. The lights were still red. She fiddled with the radio looking for music she liked. She glanced in her mirror again. It didn't look like it was going to slow down. Harriet quickly undid her seat belt and unlatched the door. At the same moment it hit her rear fender pushing the car out into a steam of fast moving traffic. Harriet rolled out straight into a mail box knocking the breath out of her lungs. She stood up to see the Chevrolet turn right amid mayhem on Foothill Drive as car after car ploughed into hers creating an explosion. She dialled 911.

"Detective Sullivan, there are multiple car wrecks at at the junction of 282 and 186. There are people injured send emergency ambulances. The crashes were caused by a green Chevrolet Tahoe now heading east on the 186. It pushed my car into crossroad traffic. This was all for my benefit, someone just tried to kill me."

It was the same for all the Homicide Detectives in the department. Sergeant Grainger Stokes was the kind of guy it was very difficult to get to know. He liked it that way. Fraternizing with the lower ranks was bad for discipline and he needed to keep them all in line. He wouldn't even talk about his wife of thirty-five years or his three grown-up children, all boys. He had worked hard to reach Sergeant and probably realized he would go no higher. Now he had the FBI on his case and he hated that. Harriet knocked and walked into his office. It was busy. Stokes was sitting at his desk on the phone while four men in suits studied maps and photographs on the wall. There stopped talking as she entered.

"Call you back," said Stokes abruptly and put the phone down. "You Ok?"

"Yeah."

"You've had a busy day Sully?"

She smiled and waved her arms as if to say so what's new and winced, touching her ribs.

"I want you to have a check over from the Doc."

"Sergeant I'm Ok."

"I wasn't asking. Close the door behind you and have a seat. Everybody grab what chairs there are. These gentlemen are FBI from the Salt Lake field office. News travels fast Detective Sullivan especially when one of our own gets targetted. We're assuming it wasn't an accidental hit and run. As you know the murder or attempted murder of a law enforcement official is a federal offence. So I want you to write a report about what just happened and send a copy to me and the local field office."

One leaned forward offering his hand, "George Briscoe, mark it for my attention." The others stayed silent.

"So what's the story about the driver of the car recovered from the river?" Stokes asked.

Harriet pulled out her notepad. "It's all a bit circumstantial but highly suspicious. Simmons was a freelance journalist. Preliminary examination of his laptop indicates he was working on a big story that I think got him killed, I don't yet know what it was or how he was killed. There are some vague references to a suspicion about contract killers that are maybe active in the State. Simmons hints that the orders are not coming from organised crime but he doesn't go into detail.

"Who are they coming from?" asked Briscoe.

"From the information we've received so far he didn't know but his wife knew he was onto something big. The key is Simmons. The attempt on my life confirms it and also the way it happened, a hit and run? An unfortunate accident? If I had died or been seriously injured where would the evidence be of murder or attempted murder?"

Stokes looked at Briscoe, put his hands together and stretched his fingers making a cracking sound.

"This is your first case Sullivan and I'm a bit worried about what happened," he said. "The attempt on your life could be for any number of reasons, and personally I don't think it's necessarily anything to do with the Simmons case. To be blunt I don't quite know what to do with you and until we find out where this attempt on you is coming from," his mobile phone rang. He looked at it and put it back in his pocket. "Ok there are options let me put them on the table. Until your partner Jeff Blackwell comes back from leave, I think you should take a back seat. You could take some leave, go on holiday or I could second you to Provo temporarily. You would still work in Homicide," he hesitated noticing Harriet's face fall.

"What about the Simmons case?"

"It's not safe for you to be in SLC right now. Wait till Jeff gets back I can't risk letting you loose until we know what's going on."

Harriet looked at the men who were watching her. "Grainger

what's this all about I don't understand did you think I might have been frightened off by a hit and run? Simmons is my case." She shook her head. "You can't take me off my first case."

He leaned forward with his hand out.

"What?"

"Your badge and your firearm."

Harriet took the badge out and placed it on the desk looking at him. "I don't carry a firearm."

"Jeez," said one of the men. "You must be the only cop in the whole country that's not armed, even Rangers in parks carry guns, what is it some kind of political point?"

"How many people have you killed?" she asked.

"A lot and they all deserved it."

"I haven't killed anyone I prefer to put criminals in prison not the morgue. Look Grainger, I'm not frightened and I need to get on and do my job. If these guys want to kill me in an obscure way they are going to have to get close to me and I'll be ready. You also have to ask yourself are you doing this because I'm a woman?"

He got out of his chair walked round the desk and leaned back on it uncomfortably close to Harriet. He slid the badge towards Harriot. "I recommended you for promotion because I believe in you and if you think that you can hack it with all this extra pressure then I can't stand in your way. I wouldn't want your first homicide to be your last." He turned to Briscoe who was studying Harriet intently. "It seems that you're already marked out Sullivan," said Grainger. "If that's the case they will know it didn't work and come after you again. They won't give up until you're dead, an accident, suicide or natural causes of course. Are you really prepared for that?"

"Yes."

"Who have you been speaking to apart from Speed?"

"Melissa the deceased's wife. He worked for most newspapers over time but laterally he concentrated on the nationals, the high payers. I tried calling a few news editors. It's not easy getting anybody today but the ones I spoke to didn't know what he was working on. They liked his exposés but not him. Some of the stings he hatched to catch people were by using hidden cameras and microphones."

Grainger stood up and walked back to his chair behind the desk. "Ok," he said pushing the badge towards her. "One condition, you're up to date with your fire arms training and from now on you carry a gun and that's a direct order."

Harriet smiled and picked it d up. "All I ask is somebody covers my back and lets me do my job. Are you sure I know everything there is to know? I don't like surprises and what are these guys going to be doing while I'm a target?"

"Go see a doctor then work in house."

"How are you feeling Harry?" Doctor Peter Marshall was scribbling away on a pad.

"Not many people call me that now Pete."

"Well I've been attending your family on and off before you were born in fact I brought you into the world, accompanied by a lusty scream I may add, I'm retiring next year. You know when I reached sixty I got lots of nice presents but I also got one unwelcome present, the cloak of invisibility. It only works on younger folks. I have to write everything down because I'm forgetting things."

"You always did have a dry sense of humour. Anyway getting back to the business in hand can we talk about me? I fell against a fire hydrant but I'm Ok, bit sore."

"Take off your jacket and top." Harriet obliged gingerly removing her shoulder holster and pistol.

"Whoa that's quite a bruise." He touched it gently. "Looks like you have three bruised ribs, take some pain killers and forget about it because there's nothing I can do even if they're cracked."

"Ok. Peter can I ask you something, hypothetically if I wanted to kill somebody without leaving any trace for a forensic pathologist to find how would I go about it?"

The Doctor raised his eyebrows. "That's not something I would normally be discussing with my patients...but seeing it's you there are many ways. Let's take poisons. Pathologists can't test for everything so for example if you choose let's say an obscure South American poison like the Amazonian Poison Dart frog? Voila perfect murder, unless the examiner was suspicious because he could test for that. Now if you didn't have access to such an exotic poison, choose one that is expected to be in the body something like Potassium. Just the right dose administered into the blood stream will do the business without being detected, result cardiac arrest. And finally my favourite. One 100 ml/s of air injected into an artery is undetectable. If you've got someone in mind we never had this conversation."

"Detective Sullivan?"

Harriet was at her desk and looked up. "Who are you?"

The evidence recovery technician looked surprised. "I'm Barry I've been working on the recovered car."

"Bit familiar aren't you?"

"It's Officer Barry."

"Oh Ok, sorry what have you got?"

Barry placed a sheaf of photographs illustrating the inside and outside at every conceivable angle. "I've been in the force a long time and this is a strange one." He hesitated. "Ok it was a three year old VW Rabbit with 32,476 miles on the clock with only four and a half gallons of gas still in the tank. The vehicle was in good shape with no faults and the tyres were all good. The doors were locked. No DNA in the car other than the victim and the victim's wife. Same with prints no third party evidence. As you can see he was still buckled up. The key was in the ignition turned to off. The steering wheel had its security lock on. There were no physical signs of the cause of death or a struggle. There were no bottles of tonic and I checked the CCTV from the store, he never got there which means the killer intercepted him before he got to the 24Seven. As I say there was no sign of a struggle."

Harriet examined the photographs while he gave his report.

"We found a mobile phone and tablet in a drawer under the passenger's chair, the tablet was full of water and I think the phone is Ok. I passed them on to IT.

"Good. I checked with the VW dealership and asked them if there is any way an electric window can be closed with the keys inside. It was a salesman they're getting back to me. Any ideas?"

He shook his head, "not a clue but it stinks to hell and high water."

"I know," said Harriet. "Simmons leaves his wife on New Year's Eve supposedly for tonic he arrives at a lonely spot next to the river and this is where the imagination kicks in. Let's say he was meeting someone he didn't want his wife to know about. Someone connected to his investigations. He was very protective of his wife she knew nothing about his work until it got published. If it is murder how was it done but more importantly why? Wouldn't it be just as simple putting a bullet in his head?

For some reason whoever it was went to great lengths to make it look like natural causes. Unfortunately if we don't find out what really happened it will end up natural causes. Thanks Barry good work."

Harriet watched him leave. She got up and went to the coffee machine and fumbled in her pocket for some coins when she heard coffee being poured.

"If I remember right, that's how you like it."

She smiled and looked up. "Hello Jack still coming to the aid of damsels in distress. What are you working on?"

"They got rid of some bad apples from Vice since they reorganized the department and there has been a huge drop in arrests, I'm told that's a good thing. We try to help the women as much as possible guiding them to the Fourth Street Clinic. They clean them up point them to help groups. But you know it's just business as usual, I'm trying to get out of it," he whispered. "Oh congratulations on your promotion by the way how about we celebrate some night?"

"How's Shirley?"

He sighed, "she doesn't understand me."

"Knock it off Jack nobody understands you."

"I've decided to make a New Year resolution. Live every day as if it were the last. What about you have you made any New Year resolutions?"

"Yeah, make a new friend a month and lose an old one," she laughed and went back to her desk.

"Weather Center? Detective Sullivan, Police Department can you tell me if there was any freak overnight weather near North Jordan River slipway…? The one, two blocks from the school… Uhu…Isn't that strange for this time of the year…Yeah thanks."

Harriet put the phone down. All of the desks were in an open plan which she disliked. Her corner had several potted plants to give her a sense of privacy. She picked up the phone again and dialled IT but there was no reply. Harriet left the room and filled a plastic cup from the water cooler as the night shift was arriving.

"Hey look who we have here, if it isn't the brand spanking newbie Detective Sullivan. Is that a new suit Sully?"

Get lost I've already done an eight hour shift today and I'm not finished yet you uniformed boys don't know you're living."

She walked down a flight of stairs and along a corridor pushing open the door of IT forensics.

Ben Pratt's eyes were shut. He was sprawled across a keyboard causing flashing alerts on the screen. Littered around him were empty cardboard and polystyrene boxes, some still with remnants of half eaten food. Harriet leaned against the door took out her phone and text him...'WAKE-UP'. Ben's phone vibrated in his pocket. He screamed took it out and flung it aside just missing Harriet and pushed himself back in his chair, raising his hand in apology.

"Sorry Sully, need a break from this room."

Harriet picked up his phone and put it on his desk. "Bad news Ben, you know whenever I come in here its more work."

"It's my partner, she's very jealous. She doesn't believe I spend so much time working here. She thinks I'm seeing someone. I'm even wearing an electronic tagging device I borrowed from Jack to convince her."

"Don't be ridiculous Ben."

"Ok, it's cool, we're good."

"How did you get on with the laptop?" she said sitting down next to a monitor.

"It's very interesting. The files you gave me were easily available almost as if he wanted them to be found and then there were several layers of encryption, this guy knew what he was doing. It put up a fight but I won."

"What's on it?"

"Hey give me a break there's a Terra byte of data on here you'll have to give me an idea what you're looking for."

"Ben just between you and me, can you make a copy of the drive and keep it in a safe place, just in case. Ok this is what I'm looking for, last use files, email addresses received and sent drafts of any articles any documents related to research especially recent ones, all photographs to be scanned by our face recognition software. I want you to contact his mobile provider triangulate his position over the last month especially its present or last known position. Check Video Link connections. I think that's enough for now. Ben I'm really sorry."

"What about?"

"I need it yesterday. I hope you don't mind working late."

"Overtime?"

"Ha, speak to the sergeant. What about the tablet and mobile found in his car."

"I only have one brain and one pair of hands, it's on the list."

Harriet almost fell asleep. She reached for the glass of red Napa Valley Trefethen taking a sip and put it back on the edge of the bath. This was a nice place to be on a cold winter's evening. She did all her best thinking in a hot bath. Of course it was nonsense for anyone to pretend Simmons had died naturally then drove the car into the river. There were only three credible possibilities.

Someone had killed him and somehow pushed the car into the water. Someone had killed and left him in the car and somehow it had ended up in the water or he died a natural death and somehow the car went into the water. When the vehicle was recovered the position it was in seemed to indicate that it had just been driven off the slip yet the key was in the ignition and it was switched off, the steering wheel was locked and the handbrake was on. What was it the weather man had said, about 4 am there was a snap thaw and then the inverse temperature kicked in again and it dropped like a stone.

"Harriet you're a genius," she said taking another sip and then her mobile rang.

She got out of the bath reluctantly and put on a white bathrobe walked through to the bedroom, picked it up and pressed the green button.

"This had better be good I've been on the go for fourteen hours today...What..? When...How...No I'll get a cab."

The cab stopped next to a forensics van near four police cars with lights flashing to be met by Detective Jeff Blackwell.

"Hey I didn't know you were back from vacation, how was Hawaii?" asked Harriet.

"I thought about joining the local force. Nancy and I were just in the door when the call came through."

"Have the department got a GPS tracker on you?"

"Probably, what's the story?"

"Well this has been a really busy day for the death of a guy with natural causes," she said.

They climbed the steps of the house and entered. Forensics was busy taking photographs of Melissa who was slumped sideways on an armchair in the living room. She had a gun clasped in her right hand and an entry wound on the side of her head.

"Her husband was fished out of Jordan River still in his car and this development makes me a whole lot more suspicious," she said.

"It looks like it may have been suicide? Maybe the shock was just too much for her." Said Jeff.

"You can check out the owner of the gun but I know it will belong to the Simmons. It's not suicide, she was left handed they're getting sloppy."

Harriet went into the kitchen and began systematically searching in a clockwise direction opening cupboards, drawers and the fridge. She opened the swing bin trash can pulled out the liner and emptied it on the floor. There was a full bottle of tonic. It didn't surprise her.

"This killing seems senseless to me. Maybe they thought she knew more than she did. Maybe they were after his computer. Sorry Jeff I've got this feeling that you've walked into something big and would you believe that there was an attempt on my life today, it's got to be linked. A sudden death with no signs of the cause, a killing dressed up as a suicide and a hit and run. It seems they are still trying to play subtle but they're getting careless. I think I've seen enough let's go back to the office and I'll bring you up to speed."

3

It was almost midnight when she had finished briefing Jeff. "Stokes assigned you to this murder and he's assigned me to her husband's murder let's work on this together, yeah? If I don't get some sleep I'll be no good tomorrow." She yawned and looked at her smart phone Home app switching on an electric blanket, choosing another app she hailed a cab. "I would really appreciate if you drop in on Ben, see how he's getting on, spend a little time and keep him on the right track. Say high to Nancy, let's all have lunch."

Harriet woke up and checked her phone, it was 8.10 am and a text read 'Meeting with the Sergeant, 10.00 am'. She hurriedly showered, dressed and called a cab. She checked her delivery box ate some toast and heard the cab outside. It arrived at Police HQ and Harriet went straight to forensic IT where Ben and Jeff were having coffee. "I've got a meeting at ten how did it go?" They looked at her windswept blond hair which was down around her shoulders.

"What?" she said.

"Nothing."

"She looked at her reflection in a blank monitor. "Oh," she said tying it up.

"I think you'll find this very interesting Sully." She sat down as he handed her a tablet and read it carefully.

"This guy had a death wish alright. He most certainly wasn't stupid just brave. I see him in a new light. Come with me Jeff, where's the meeting?"

"I'll come but this is really your show, I'm only back five minutes. It's in briefing room five."

"Good work guys. Ben you're a star go home and say hello to your partner do you want a note."

He smiled, "she knows, she's used to it."

"Can I hang on to this for the meeting?"

"That's what it's for."

"Who's on the next shift?"

"No-one. They've been looking for a replacement for Grant but no luck so far."

Some people were still arriving at the briefing room when they entered. Jeff sat down as Harriet linked her tablet to the large monitor on the wall. The Sergeant walked in with a sheaf of papers and a coffee and stood at the head of table.

"Detective Sullivan these guys are observers from the CIA, NSA, Homeland Security and you'll remember Special Agent George Briscoe from the FBI."

There was a tense silence. Harriet looked around the room, she had everyone's attention.

"Joseph Gideon Simmons was a very clever and very brave investigative journalist. His wife said he had received and replied to a couple of texts. He made an excuse to his wife ostensibly to go to a 24Seven mart for a bottle of tonic but he actually left the house to meet someone he knew..."

"How do you know that?"

"He didn't go to the 24Seven...CCTV confirms that and there was an unopened bottle of tonic in his kitchen trash can so we can deduce that he didn't want his wife to know what he was doing. He was found dead in his car in the Jordan River with no signs of foul play, windows closed, doors locked. I believe he was murdered, how I don't know yet. What got my attention but at the same time complicated the investigation was that the car went into the river with the handbrake on, the ignition switched off and the steering locked. There were no tracks down the slipway. Now a crane could have been used but there was no indication of stress or marks on the bodywork. Having checked with the National Weather Service, there was a dramatic change in the temperature during the early morning of New Year's Day at approximately 4.00 am. So what happened to the car on an icy incline when the ice started to melt? It gently slid down and off the slipway into the water. Then according to the Weather Centre there were showers of sleet and snow and the temperature plummeted again covering up the cause and the tracks. So we know how the car ended up in the river. Preliminary autopsy cites natural causes because the coroner couldn't find any evidence of wrongdoing but I repeat I believe he was murdered. I'm waiting for the results of a full autopsy. Last night his wife was found dead in her living room with a single shot to the head with the family's own pistol. We may have got to Mrs Simmons before the killers because I believe they were after the laptop. But they made a mistake. When Melissa Simmons wrote her husbands' mobile number for me she used her left hand but whoever shot her, put the weapon in her right hand."

Harriet stopped to take a sip from a glass of water and turned to look at the screen.

"Forensics has examined in detail Simmons laptop and I'll come to that in a minute. Firstly having checked with the phone company's triangulation of his phone, Simmons movements over the last three months indicates he was in the midst of two on-going investigations which may well have been linked. He spent time in and around locations of interest specifically the headquarters of two multinational corporations. Universal Defence and Development Contractors Corporation and Bailey and Bailey International Commodities Broker Incorporated, one of the biggest commodity brokers in the US..."

"...Detective where is this taking us?"

Harriet stopped and looked at the questioner bemused and scratched an ear.

"Thank you for your patience gentlemen would you like me to continue or have you heard enough?" There was silence. "That particular model of VW may have had an ability to close an electric window while the key is still in the ignition on the off position. The last known location from both tablet and phone was where his car was found and further inspection of the car revealed them to be hidden in a well under his seat His phone was one of the latest waterproof types but the tablet needs drying out. The calls list made and received from his phone confirms the investigations and some of the calls he received were made from this building. So I believe he was receiving or giving information to or from SLCPD. Someone on the force knew what he was doing before he was killed and presumably what the line of enquiry was about. Turning to the laptop. There are early very sketchy draft pieces written on both companies all speculation and circumstantial and I hesitate to go into detail at this stage with Sergeant Stokes permission. Somewhere out there is a copy of his finished expose`. It appears that Simmons believed that these two companies illegally conspired together to gain advantage over rivals. He hints at the possibility that in their determination to succeed they might have used third party contractors to silence dissenters or indeed anyone that may have stumbled on to their operations. I believe his plan was to publish one after the other to maximize the impact in the media to keep it running and the first one was due to be released. Face recognition scanning of his clandestine photographs has highlighted a number of individuals who worked for these companies and some others who are not known to us." Six well-built mercenary types flashed up on the screen. "Perhaps databases from the NSA might track them down. I've issued an alert on highway and City CCTV scanning cameras to see if they show up. In summary we know Melissa Simmons was murdered, we know there was a clear cut motive to have Joe Simmons killed. If you are knowledgeable enough there are many ways to kill without trace." Harriet sat down amid a murmur around the room.

"Harriet." Grainger stood up. "I'd like to thank you for all that hard work and some of you here may not know that there was an attempt on Detective Sullivan's life yesterday."

"If I may," George Briscoe stood up. "This investigation is too big for one person. Can I suggest that Detective's Sullivan and Blackwell concentrate on those responsible for the killings while the FBI investigates these companies?"

"Makes sense to me," said Stokes. Copies of Detective Sullivan's report will be circulated for those who need to know. Any questions...?" He didn't wait for any. "Thank you. Harriet, Jeff stay for a moment."

When everybody had filed out Grainger looked up from the papers on the table.

"Jeff could you get us three fresh coffees put it on expenses." He looked at Harriet and left.

"Close the door Sully. That was a fine case presentation, I'm proud of you. This is between you and me nobody else. Let Jeff go after the contract killers he'll get plenty backup, officially you will be working on that as well. Ok we know they killed Mr and Mrs Simmons what we don't know is who else did they kill but also and more importantly we don't know who was feeding info to Joe Simmons from here and who is helping these killers get away with it. They must have had specialized help. Check out the suicides, accidental deaths, natural causes and missing persons. They may have made more mistakes like Mrs Simmons. I want you to find out who they are and try cross referencing Simmons calls to who was on duty here at the time. If there were a number of calls it might throw up an individual."

"Grainger, I know what you're doing. Are you sure you're not just keeping me out of the way safe and sound for a while?" she said smiling.

"Don't get too smart. Macho men don't dig smart women," he said pointing at her with a stubby finger, "anyway it's not very becoming."

Harriet's phone sounded an alert, she opened it clicked on home smart and an image of two masked men with guns was searching her house.

"Grainger two armed intruders in my house right now."

He picked up the phone. "There's a 10-86 at 1206 University Boulevard Court, 10-40, I repeat 10-40. Extreme caution, 10-30 I repeat 10-30."

"10-4." Came the reply over the radio. "10-23, I repeat 10-23."

Harriet linked her phone to the monitor on the screen horrified as the search went on. "How did they get in? What on earth are they looking for?"

One checked upstairs as the other one went in to a small study and fired up her computer. He took out a memory stick and plugged it in. The computer was waiting for a user passphrase.

"Wait," Harriet wound up the audio and made a split screen

showing upstairs and downstairs.

"They're trying a brute force attack to get the password," said Grainger. "That could take them a bit of time. How many characters in your password?

"Seven."

"That might buy us enough time. See what I mean about always carrying a gun? Listen to me next time."

"How long before rapid response gets there?"

Grainger looked at his watch. "Six minutes."

"He's in my bedroom pulling out all my drawers and emptying them on the floor. Give us a break. There's nothing in the Ottoman, stop pulling out the blankets. What are they looking for?"

"He's still waiting to crack your password."

The door burst open and with shouts of police a barrage of gunfire rang out catching them by surprise. They fired back and died under a hail of police bullets crashing against furniture leaving bloodstains on the wall.

"Lucky you weren't at home, or maybe they knew you weren't at home."

"Harriet felt sick. I can't stay there tonight," she said.

"Of course you can't it's a crime scene. We may have some leads for your partner. There's VIP accommodation here you can use." Harriet was putting her mobile phone into a pocket. "What do you think you're doing with that, come on hand it over its evidence. We'll get you another one."

What about a car I can't keep getting cabs?"

"Talk to the car pool manager."

"Oh about accommodation thanks for the offer I spend too much time here as it is. I think I might stay the night with Jeff and Nancy, sort something out tomorrow."

"Get yourself a dog, a large fierce one with big teeth and a loud bark..."

"...and spend all my time picking up dog poo and apologising to the neighbours for the noise, no thanks I'd rather get shot."

4

"ID."

Harriet took out her badge and showed it to the car pool manager. "And you are...?"

"Graham, You're lucky I'm here they've got me double shifting. It's always the same this time of year guys off sick without any warning. I can't go off sick I'm the car pool manager. But it means I'm running around doing the job of four guys...crazy. What can I do for you?"

"Well Graham, I need a car. This is a really small office."

"It's not an office it's a booth. I don't spend all my time in here. My office whenever I can get to it is upstairs. Are you the one that wrote off your car at some traffic lights."

"No someone else managed to do that for me, what have you got?"

"Not very much," he said looking at a list. "We're kind of short just now, waiting for a new delivery. Hey I've got an idea why don't you come up and I'll show you my office? It's much more comfortable and private."

"Don't get fresh with me pal." She winced as a pain shot across her ribs. "I don't care just give me whatever you've got. I'll take anything."

"Ok. Your loss." He reached up and took down a set of keys and handed them to Harriet. "Bay F51. Over to the right."

"Thanks...*Graham*."

"Are you ready to order Sully?" asked Jan pouring coffee into her cup, "nice wheels."

"Thanks," Harriet said drily. Jan's Diner was almost empty. Sitting at a corner table through police habit, Ben and Jeff had already ordered.

"Wheels what wheels?" asked Ben.

"Oh nothing, meatloaf please Jan and a salad." She went off to get the order. "Did the uniforms have to shoot up my house like that? I bet they were enjoying themselves, what a mess."

Ben stood up and looked out of the window. He sat down with a big smirk. "A Humvee?" he snorted. "Graham's been trying to offload that Humvee onto homicide for years," he said picking up the Gazette.

"You know he tried hitting on me. I could've put the cuffs on him and arrested him for sexual harassment."

"Cuffs," said Ben. "Yea Graham would've enjoyed that."

Jeff seemed troubled and was busy texting someone.

"Who's going to pay for all the damage Jeff?"

Harriet looked at him and he carried on avoiding her gaze. She made it more obvious by leaning forward putting her elbow on the table resting her chin on the palm of her hand. Their eyes met.

"What are you doing?" he asked.

"What's wrong?"

"Nothing."

"I can get another table if you two want to be alone," said Ben.

"Coffees? When was the last time Grainger ask me to get coffees? and put them on expenses, what's that all about I'd get laughed off the force if I did that."

"After what happened this morning, can I stay the night?"

Ben looked over his newspaper. "Listen I was actually joking but this is sounding serious guys. Wizen up you two. Jeff you've got a lovely wife get a grip and stop this nonsense."

"Of course you can but don't mention this morning to Nancy, she'll freak out."

"Freak out, freak out, are you two nuts of course she'll freak out."

Harriet looked at him. "Ben what are you babbling about?"

"One meatloaf and salad, one double burger with onions and fries and chicken with fries, enjoy."

"You changed the subject you're always doing that to me. Why was I sent out for coffee?"

"Listen Jeff let me ask you something, if you were given privileged information from the Sergeant would you feel honour bound to keep it confidential?"

"I suppose so, are we still partners?"

"Will you two knock it off?"

"Of course. I'm going through a list of John Does, suicides accidents and missing persons. It might throw up a pattern. This afternoon I'm going to get Ben here to try constructing some algorithms. Satisfied?"

"Good," he said looking away embarrassed, "good."

Ben's tech lab had been tidied up a little after complaints by the early morning cleaning crew. It had been used by forensics before he took it over and remnants of their equipment had been left behind. All manner of jars and bottle lined a shelf under an internal glazed window. The large table in front of a large window with Venetian blinds drawn had six monitors on it linked to an equal number of computers.

"I can't believe it Ben, there are on average 557 successful suicides every year in Utah and over 3,300 admissions to hospitals with attempted suicide. It's an epidemic. You could easily hide a dozen murders and nobody would have time to even check them properly. That's appalling. We have the highest rates of suicide in the US and the most common method is suffocation. Suffocation what does that even mean?"

"Hanging," he said chewing on a bagel. "Ok I can't beat that but it's still appalling there were 214 fatalities due to car crashes in 2015. So I can't find records of non-vehicular accidental deaths and I don't have stats for missing persons in Utah but there are almost half a million people in the US who go missing that are not likely to be found. If you break that down to a likely statistical figure for Utah I guestimate that to be around 20,000 people go missing in Utah every year. I could be wrong."

"Let's deal with what we can deal with, suicides and accidental deaths. Can you write an algorithm that might throw up an anomaly from the database starting with suicides that may have a link with the two companies in question? Forget the attempts."

"I thought FBI was dealing with them."

"They are. If we get information useful to them we'll most likely pass it on."

Nancy took a great pride in her cooking although she rarely measured anything accurately. Throwing in bits of this, splashes of that, sprinkles of seasoning, adding a couple of twists of pepper it never tasted the same but it always tasted good. Her speciality by nationality was anything Italian which was hardly surprising since her grandmother came for Napoli. The red and white chequered table cloth was covered in dishes, appetizers, garlic bread, various pastas and of course the obligatory Bolognese sauce.

"I've been hearing rumours," she said glancing at Harriet while toying with her spaghetti.

Jeff put his fork down. "It was only a one night fling honest nothing serious, we both had a little too much to drink and..."

"...shut up idiot, you know what I mean. Harry is it true that someone tried to kill you yesterday?"

Nancy and Harriet had been high school friends long before she met Jeff. He was uncomfortable with the conversation.

"Yes."

"Is it connected to the case you're on?"

"Nancy? said Jeff.

Harriet put her hand on Jeff's arm. "Yes, well I think so but we're making progress and it's a big operation with a lot of Intel and a lot of resources. Don't worry Nancy the bad guys never win."

"Let's change the subject," he said.

"Ok is there anybody on the horizon?" asked Nancy.

"There's a shrimp of a car pool manager that tried hitting on me. Never even met him before. I've given up on guys just now I thought I'd give them a rest for a while, I'm hopeless I always pick the wrong kind, maybe you should do the picking for me, what do you think Jeff? Would it be Ok if Nancy and I went on the hunt, for me I mean?"

"I'm sorry I seem to have," He moved his jaw a couple of times. "Lost my hearing."

"I was in the Morgue yesterday. In between Latin phrases speedy was to say the least very uncomplimentary, did the macho why don't you go home and have babies?"

"What? You should file a complaint. What did you say?"

"File a complaint nah there was nobody else there"

Nancy poured a little more red wine into Harriet and Jeff's glass. "You know Jeff when Harry and I were at high school…" Harriet rolled her eyes. "…She was a guy magnet and oblivious. The campus was strewn with broken hearts and awash with tears no kidding, Harry would blithely walk all over them. These poor saps would try hitting on me just to get close to Harry."

"Is that true Sully?" he said.

"I don't know about that however…let me see," Harriet sipped the wine. "At high school Nancy was quite keen on this geeky boy with sticky out teeth and thick glasses but I believe his folks were loaded at least that was the only explanation that I could think of at the time…"

"…Ok, Ok truce."

Harriet waved her fork in the air looking at Nancy. "You've changed. Have you done something to your hair? Could be the holiday you've just had in Hawaii, you always took on a nice colour. No, it's not that I've allowed for that. You know there's definitely something different about you, a flush of colour to the cheeks a sparkle in the eye, a little excitement bubbling away and you're not drinking alcohol. Now my dear Watson what would you deduce from that? Because to me it's ele-bloody-mentary."

"You're getting too smart." Said Nancy giving Jeff a dig in the ribs. "I told you we wouldn't be able to keep it from Harry."

"Really! Fantastic, it was actually a shot in the dark." She got up and gave them both a kiss on the cheek. "That's wonderful news congratulations, wow. I'm going to have to get cracking now I've got a bit of catching up to do. When's the baby due?"

"August the thirtieth."

"I'm so pleased. Is it still too early to tell if it's a boy or a girl?"

"No, but we don't want to know, let's keep it a surprise," she said holding Jeff's hand. "As long as the baby's healthy we don't care."

"Can I be Godmother?"

"Of course Harry we were going to ask you anyway, we'd be honoured."

The evening wore on as the conversation moved on to people they knew that they hadn't seen for some time. Past memories, shared jokes until Harriet yawned.

"Listen would you mind if I hit the sack, I haven't had much sleep in the last twenty-four hours and if I don't I'll be sleeping in my spaghetti. Oh Nancy, do you own a gun?"

"What? What would I need a gun for working at a law firm? If I did I'd only end up accidentally shooting myself."

Jeff and Harriet's exchanged glances that spoke volumes yet they said nothing. Harriet's phone rang. "Hello Ben...clever you... wait, Ben's got a face match on one of the guys from Simmons laptop; I'll pass you over Jeff's handling that."

Harriet gave the phone to Jeff who left the room.

"Thanks for having me Nancy, I'll move back tomorrow once the crime prevention guys check out how they got in and increase security."

"You can stay as long as you like...whoa wait a minute, what? Who got in where? Why? What happened?"

"Sorry did I just say that, I'm tired it must have just slipped out. My house was broken into today but I think they were more interested in hacking into my computer."

Jeff came back.

"Jeff you didn't tell me that Harry's house was broken into."

He looked at Harriet.

"Just slipped out," she said.

He sat down. "We didn't want to worry you, it's all under control. Ben's got a great lead. I'll have to go in."

Nancy began clearing the dishes away helped by Harriet.

"Will you two be Ok?" asked Jeff.

"Of course," said Nancy.

5

Harriet was in a deep sleep. She could hear a phone ringing in the distance getting louder. She opened her eyes. The room was completely unfamiliar she looked over and picked it up remembering where she was. It was 5.25am.

"Jeff...Ok...No I'll come over...Good work the pair of you." Harriet got dressed and left quietly.

"Who is he?"

"Paviel Dashkevich, born in Minsk in 1970. The FSB and the Belarus State Security Committee are looking for him.

"How did you catch him?" Harriet was looking at a screen.

"Parking lot with real time face recognition cameras. It triggered an alert in time for us to get there to meet him when he came back for his car."

"What about associates?"

"There's at least twelve unaccounted for all ex State Security Committee."

"Whoa wait a sec, I'm worried about what's going on here Jeff did you decide to bring him in?"

"No Sully I was dead against it. We could have put a tracker on the vehicle. It was on the orders of the Sergeant."

"Sergeant Stokes?" Jeff nodded. "Really that's strange. So the contractors are from Belarus," said Harriet.

"Well this one is, we don't know about the others yet. I've called for an interpreter. He had no identification on him, no papers, no drivers licence, no money, no credit cards. All he had was a piece of paper with an address and a small pistol hidden inside his boot. That's exactly the same drill as the two that broke into your house. The address he had on him is 2304 South Main Street, Central Business District."

"What's there?"

"It's a twenty floor office block with each floor having a different business apart from the top two floors let to Gerrard Associates & Co who are one of the biggest hedge fund managers in the US with over a trillion dollars of assets under management."

"You've done a great job guys, I'm proud of you. There is one question that sticks out like a sore thumb though..." She was stopped in her tracks.

"...The answer is yes there is a connection with Gerrard Associates, at least one of the companies being investigated. Bailey and Bailey International Commodities Broker Incorporated staged a hostile takeover and failed at the last minute Gerrard's CEO sabotaged it."

Jeff and Harriet were led into a holding cell that was also an interview room. With a bed against one wall, a table in the middle with three chairs and one of them fixed to the floor holding their prisoner. His hands handcuffed behind him were looped through the steel top rail. He was built like a heavyweight wrestler, all muscle. He had a shaven head, a dark beard and wore a checked shirt with dirty blue jeans. He had an air of confidence as an untouchable would, staring straight ahead. Jeff and Harriet sat at the other side of the table, Jeff looked at some notes while Harriet studied him. Someone had said to her once that within seconds of meeting a stranger a huge amount of conscious and subconscious information pass between them but she had met a brick wall. He was passive and cocky with it. There was no fear no anxiety, just patiently waiting, but for what?

"Do you speak English?" asked Jeff. "You're being held here on suspicion of being an illegal immigrant and illegal possession of a firearm. What's your name? Who are you working for?" There was the hint of a smirk from him.

The door opened, it was the desk Sergeant with an interpreter.

"Stokes wants to see the pair of you."

Harriet knocked and they entered.

"Dashkevich's lawyer is at reception, he wants to see his client," said Stokes.

Harriet winced. "He's an illegal alien. He is in possession of an unlicensed firearm. He has no papers no identification. He deliberately has nothing that can identify him which means he was on a mission when he was picked up same as the guys in my house. Have they been identified yet?" Grainger shook his head. "Who's the lawyer?"

"Harold Skinner."

"With your permission Grainger I'll deal with it. Jeff go back down and take somebody with you. See if the interpreter can get anything out of him." When they had gone Harriet turned and looked at the Sergeant. "What's going on Grainger?"

He looked uncomfortable. "Just do your job Sully." She stood looking at him with her arms folded.

"Get out of here."

Harriet held her ground. "Someone not a million miles away

from this office once said to me all the best clinical detective work in the world can't compete with a sound knowledge and understanding of the human psyche. Sound familiar? I've known you for a long time. You are what I aspire to be so what the heck is going on."

Grainger drummed his short podgy fingers on the desk and stood up. "The decision was taken to pull in Dashkevich higher up against my advice. It came from Deputy Chief Bingham."

"Why didn't you say so? You had me worried there. That cocky guy downstairs knows he's protected. Are you happy for me to deal with this dodgy lawyer?" Grainger waved her away and sat down.

Harold Skinner was a naturally thin man with bird –like features. He had a pointy chin and a thin long nose that he frequently used for emphasis. He was studying a document when he saw Harriet striding towards him.

"Mr Skinner, Detective Sullivan what can I do for you." The reception was noisy and busy. "Why don't we go in here?" She led him in to a small interview room. "Have a seat would you like a coffee?"

"No thank you, I would like to see my client."

"Oh? What's your climates name?"

"His name is Paviel Dashkevich."

"That's curious," she said, "because we do not have anyone in our cells answering to that name, I'm sorry. Now since we have not met before can you provide me with proof that you are a qualified practising lawyer? Which practice are you with?"

"What?"

Harriet sat there arms folded with a fixed stare. He handed over a card. "Anyone can print cards." She said pushing it back.

"I work for Brotherton, Raymond & Associates. The Sergeant can vouch for me."

"I don't accept vouchers either Mr Skinner can you excuse me a minute?"

Harriet got up and left the room. She took her phone out. "Ben, can you check to see if any of the companies currently in this investigation use Brotherton, Raymond & Associates, call back."

Mr Skinner was still sitting at the desk looking bewildered when Harriet came back. He had never been treated like this before.

"Mr Skinner who or what leads you to believe that we are holding your client?"

"I'm sorry client confidentiality."

"If you are in possession..." Harriet's phone rang. "Excuse me... yes...Ok thanks. If you are in possession of and withholding evidence to a crime then that is a criminal offence and the law applies equally to me as it does to you. There is no one being held here that claims to be the person you named as your client. Now is there anything you wish to tell me?"

Skinner looked at her in disbelief then stood up. "You have no idea what you are dealing with here Detective Sullivan," he said with a thin smile and a nod. "I'm sure our paths will cross again and hopefully next time with a more productive outcome."

"Oh by the way I understand that your clientele includes Universal Defence and Development Contractors Corporation and Bailey and Bailey International Commodities Broker Incorporated?"

"We have many clients Detective Sullivan. You take care."

6

Harriet was in her office eating a smoked salmon and cream filled bagel from the canteen while she poured over both Joseph and Melissa Simmons autopsies when the door opened and Jeff came in.

"Look at this." She tapped on Simmons file. "Speedy found nothing on Simmons...he sticks to the death by natural causes. Has your man said anything yet?" she said.

"No, how did you get rid of Skinner?"

"I asked him for his credentials his eyes nearly popped out of his head and I told him no one in the cells answered to the name of Dashkevich which of course is true. Skinner was a little bit threatening when he left. This Simmons autopsy stinks I can't believe he found nothing. Speedy's missing something I know it. What do I do Jeff? I don't want Joe Simmons death marked down as natural."

"We could get a second opinion."

"Are you kidding, talk about rattling cages I don't want to make enemies, it's easier making enemies than friends. Have you got Dashkevich's file. Is there anything new about him?"

"Yeah a little bit, it's on here." He passed her the tablet.

"Let's go and speak to mystery man."

There were four police in the cell watching Dashkevich eat when they came in.

"I hope the food is to your liking Mr Dashkevich," said Harriet finishing her bagel and sitting down, "we know quite a bit about you." He looked up in surprise. "We know your English is good. Is there anyone you would like us to contact on your behalf? No? Minsk must be very cold this time of the year, I hope your family is keeping warm. Well we can't keep you here indefinitely of course, you will either be extradited to Minsk or Moscow which would you prefer? We know you were just about to fulfil a contract and your friends must be getting concerned about you. So far, entering the country illegally and carrying a concealed weapon isn't insurmountable as far as any potential understanding between us might progress to. Do you understand? Of course you do. I don't have the authority to conclude a deal but my recommendations are listened to." She picked at a piece of food stuck between her teeth. "We're not interested in you but you would serve a term in prison perhaps a year or two after which we could put you on any plane you like and you would see Katya again. She's very pretty. How old is she nine? Think about it Mr Dashkevich but not too long things can change very quickly and you won't get a better offer." They stood up and looked down at him. He hadn't raised his head since his name was spoken out loud.

"Wait," he growled. Jeff and Harriet looked at each other then the door burst open.

"Upstairs," said Grainger.

They walked through the corridor up a flight of stairs two at a time along another corridor into homicide and entered his office.

"I've just had Bingham on the phone he wants you in his office."

"Dashkevich was just about to talk."

Grainger was pacing around the room. He stopped and turned. "Are you still here."

As they left the office Jeff caught Harriet's elbow. "I'm coming as well."

"There's no time for heroics go back down and speak to Dashkevich, take some official looking papers necessary for passports visas etc. Make it look like you're getting the paper work ready and wire yourself up so he doesn't get spooked. I'll play for time. Go."

The atmosphere was ice cold. They sat there with all eyes on Harriot waiting for the fireworks to start.

"Come in Detective. Sullivan," said Bingham breaking the silence. "Please take a seat. You've met Mr Skinner and you'll know of course Assistant District Attorney Bradley Hooper."

Harriot nodded amiably.

"Now since you are the case officer we don't want to ride rough shod all over it but we would like everyone who is held in our cells to be properly represented by legal counsel when requested."

Deputy Chief Bingham had clearly spent far too much time sitting behind a desk. He looked on edge and his eyes darted around the room, but the others avoided his glances.

"I couldn't agree with you more sir," she said

"Good, good. You have in custody Mr Paviel Dashkevich?"

"No sir as I said, we have no-one who answers to that name. Now I have a John Doe who refuses to speak, who has not requested a lawyer and until I can confirm his identity he remains John Doe but I'm intrigued sir. How is it that a lawyer is in possession of information that may help solve a crime I mean Mr Skinner appears to be asserting that the man in custody is his client when we are not even certain as to his identity. I have already cautioned Mr Skinner about with-holding information evidential in a criminal case. The suspect held by us has been arrested for entering the country illegally and possessing an unlicensed firearm. So as I understand it as an illegal immigrant he has no rights for anyone to represent?"

"It's Harriet isn't it?" asked Hooper.

Harriet smiled sweetly.

"I've heard great things about you and I've been seriously impressed. You see, we have a very complicated situation. There is a, shall I say, a much bigger picture that needs to be addressed."

"I thank you sir. Not being privy to the bigger picture makes my job a whole easier and I am just trying to do the job that I have been trained to do."

A silence ensued. Harriet wasn't backing down and Bingham wasn't making a strong enough case for Skinner to have access to Dashkevich.

"Perhaps Mr Skinner might be of some assistance and identify John Doe," said Hooper.

"If he is my client I would like some time alone to advise him of his rights."

"What does he look like?"

"Excuse me?"

"Give me a description?"

Skinner turned his back on Harriet and looked at the Deputy Chief.

"Mr Skinner with the greatest respect. It appears this man has entered the country illegally. He is not an American citizen, he has no rights. You would of course have to supply documentation to my satisfaction that John Doe is Dashkevich before you could act on his behalf."

Bingham was sweating. Hooper was tapping his teeth with a pencil.

"Gentlemen can you excuse me I still have two homicides that are linked and need my attention. I believe there will be more."

"How did it go?" Harriet was making her way down to the cells and bumped into Jeff. "He wants to speak to you; I think he might be ready to talk."

Harriet poured a couple of cups of strong black coffee from the machine and entered the cell followed by Jeff and three burly officers. Dashkevich was doing press-ups on the floor and got up. Harriet put the cups on the table and took a seat alongside Jeff. Dashkevich sat down and looked at her.

"Do you smoke?" he nodded. She looked at the officers. "Come on guys."

One of them took out a pack and tossed it on the table. Dashkevich took one out and looked at the officer. He came forward lit it and stepped back. Dashkevich inhaled deeply and coughed blowing out the smoke, carefully watched by Harriet. Then there was a long period of silence. It was the classic interrogation technique. Using tension in the atmosphere, there was no need for questioning not just yet. He put his left hand over his brow hiding his eyes and took another draw on the cigarette that made it glow fiercely. His hands were rough and calloused like a labourer or a farm worker with dirty nails. He had a letter in Cyrillic tattooed on the back of each finger. He took the cap off the polystyrene coffee cup, poured a little coffee in it, took another out of the pack and lit it with the almost finished cigarette then stubbed it out on the lid. He drank some coffee and raised his eyes to meet Harriet's.

"My name is Paviel Gregor Dashkevich. Just like you have your job, I have mine. I kill people and I'm good at it. It doesn't matter to me who or what the target is once the contract is issued it's just business. You are very lucky to be alive, for how long I don't know if I had the contract you would be dead by now." he shrugged, leaned back with his cigarette in his mouth and put his hands behind his head looking up. "We all die...eventually." He said putting his arms down and looked at her. "If you send me back I will be tortured," he said casually. "I'm not afraid. A violent death for me is inevitable, you can only die once." He took another drag from the cigarette and stubbed it out. "I don't want anything from you for me. Katya is ten years old and lives alone with her grandmother in Troitskoye Predmestye, Trinity Suburb. It's in the old town of Minsk. My mother is dying, Katya has no one else. This was to be my last contract and then I was to take care of her."

"What is it you want Mr Dashkevich?"

"There are people who would use her to get to me, bad people. I want you to fly Katya to me. When she arrives I will tell you everything I know even though I know my name will go on the list. If anything happens to me put her in a foster home under another name," he shrugged. "I trust you will keep your word. There is nowhere safe, not even here."

Harriet passed a piece of paper to him. "Write a letter to your grandmother explaining someone will be picking up Katya and write down her address." She stood up watching him finish and took the letter nodded then left followed by Jeff. They went to her desk behind the pot plants. Harriet sat down while Jeff paced the floor. He stopped looked at her and shook his head.

"I'm speechless. You hardly said anything. You're a genius."

The adrenalin was coursing through her veins. "Right, I'd better go and see Grainger, coming?"

He smiled, "no Harriet you don't need me I've got work to do."

Harriet heard the Grainger call out when she knocked on his door. She went in but he wasn't alone.

"I'll come back," she said.

"No come in Sully these guys are just leaving." He stood up and shook hands and they looked at her as they left. "Sit down Sully, what have you got?" Harriet stayed by the open door with her hands on her hips. "Ok, what's going on?" he asked.

"Can we go somewhere, Jan's Diner is across the road. She does some amazing stuffed bagels. I feel like some fresh air."

Grainger recognised the expression on her face, that said, I'm not telling you here. He got up and put on his coat. "Ok, your tab."

The Diner was unusually busy. Harriet chose her usual table in the corner. "Sully, you're in early," Jan said pouring out coffee, "ready to order darlin?"

"I'd like a bagel with a surprise filling."

Jan sighed, "sparrow food. What about you Grainger, don't see you in here much?"

"A piece of cake. No maybe not, I don't know, anything." Grainger watched her go and turned to look at Harriet. "What's with all the cloak and dagger Sully?"

"Dashkevich is willing to talk but he wants to do a deal…"

"…Why bring me over here?"

"The only people I trust is you, Ben from IT and Jeff. Dashkevich has a young daughter in Minsk. He won't talk until she is flown to America. In return he'll tell us everything he knows."

"And what does he know?"

Harriet took a sip of coffee. "A lot more than we do."

"I can't authorise it, needs to be higher up."

"I know that's what worries me."

"What do you mean?"

"Nothing that can't keep. Grainger we need clearance on this and quick."

"Surprise bagel and surprise cake. Enjoy," said Jan moving away quickly.

"What do you call this?" asked Grainger poking at it.

Harriet smiled. "It's a dream ring, how sweet. I on the other hand have a wonderful prawn and cream cheese filling with garlic and lemon."

Grainger pushed it aside. "How much time have we got to get a decision?"

Harriet had a mouthful of bagel. She looked at her watch. "An hour?"

"Heck Sully do you think I have a magic wand?"

"Come on this is a break through. It could crack the whole case wide open. The first thing we need to do is get him to a safe house with a swat guard."

"Look Sully there's no shortcut, I have to go through the Chief and the DA."

"You don't need me for that I have to get on."

Grainger stood up. "Thanks for the coffee."

7

"Here thought you might like this."

Dashkevich picked it up. "What is it?"

"A dream ring of course. I've put a request upstairs. I don't see any problem Paviel."

Chunks of cream stuck to his beard as he ate. "I'm very grateful, thank you."

"Paviel I know we've got a deal but generally speaking, how much do you know?"

"Everything. Who the contractors are, where they are, the corporate contacts who issue the contracts, the targets and more much more way beyond crooked businessmen and hit men."

Harriet looked at Jeff and back at Paviel. "I give you my word that even if anything should happen to you, Katya will come to America even if I have to go and get her myself. I'm very worried that something will happen to you before Katya gets here, do you trust me?"

"No," he said wiping his beard."

"Well I trust you but I need something. Look I'm doing my best here, I know they're going to come back and say how can we trust him? I need something."

"Bring me a pen, a piece of paper and an envelope. You will open this only in the event of my death or the arrival of Katya. Now I trust you."

He started writing. Harriet held her breath. Eventually he finished folding the two sheets of paper placing them in the envelope and sealing it. He then wrote his name on the envelope and handed it to Harriet. She looked at it and slipped it behind the cover of her tablet.

"Paviel just to ensure that my promise to you is kept, no one else will know about this."

"Now what happens next?" he said.

"We're moving you to a safe house, here wear this you'll need it." She handed him a duvet jacket.

Jeff came over to Harriet's desk. "Sully are you completely off your head? This is crazy. You're taking a huge risk. If anybody finds out you have that on you you'll either be killed by the bad guys or arrested for with-holding evidence. You've got to hand that into Grainger."

Harriet was shaking as she found a bigger envelope and took out Paviel's envelope. "I gave Paviel my word and Grainger didn't. I'm not taking that risk. I know what I'm doing Jeff, I'm not stupid I have the answer. Where is the safest place for this document?" Jeff shrugged, "in SLCPD Property and Evidence Bureau. I'll file it under, and remember this, 'Melissa Miscellaneous,' Ok?"

Jeff shook his head as she slipped it in and marked, dated and sealed it. "Sully...Harriet there is an unspoken understanding between me and Nancy that I will always look out for you, no matter how difficult you make it for me," he said leaning against her desk.

Harriet handed him the envelope and kissed him on the cheek as Ben walked into Homicide.

"For gawd's sake will you two pack it in," he shook his head.

"Your poor wife Jeff."

"Will you lodge this for me Jeff? Ben get yourself a coffee and hang out here for five minutes I need to see Grainger."

Harriet walked through the open plan desks knocked on his door and walked in. He was on the phone and beckoned her in. She sat down and waited trying not to listen to the one sided conversation.

"Sully congratulations, the Chief and the DA have agreed."

Harriet fished out the letter and the address and gave it to Grainger. "This is a letter that will explain the situation to Dashkevich's grandmother. The sooner the little girl is here the quicker we move. So when do we move him to a safe house."

"Right now."

"I'd like to come Grainger."

"Ok."

Harriet went back to her desk where Ben was sitting drinking coffee. "Ben I'm sorry I have to go, what have you got?"

"Interesting stuff, wait a sec I'll transfer it to your tablet Ok?"

"When Jeff comes back will you tell him I'm taking Dashkevich to a safe house."

"Gone, Barney what do you mean gone?" Harriet couldn't believe it.

"Four FBI agents showed up and took him away."

"Did they show you ID?" Barney looked away. "You didn't check their ID, Barney!" Harriet ran up the stairwell from the cells into the office where Jeff and Dan were talking. "Paviel's gone. He's been taken by four men claiming to be FBI, they didn't show

Barney any ID. Ben did you install the GPS tracker in the jacket?"

"Of course."

"Good it may save his life. Tune it into my tablet, Jeff come with me." They went through to the Sergeant's office knocked on the door and went in. "Grainger, somebody took Dashkevich without authorisation but we can find him with a tracker."

Harriet took out her phone. "Ben lock on to Dashkevich's signal and punch it through to Grainger. Launch the large drone and link it up to its transmission. Grainger I'm going after him I'll call for back up when I need it." She called Jeff. "Meet me in the parking lot right away."

Within minutes they were pursuing the signal from Dashkevich's tracker with Jeff at the wheel.

Harriet tapped her phone. "Grainger don't intercept they might lead us to the contractors, we've got the signal and we're in pursuit. Don't use any police frequencies. Hello, hello Ben can you link the image from the drone to me...Ok...where...I get it." Up came an image of a large black people carrier with blacked-out windows travelling past Temple Square. "Now we know what they look like. Grainger put Rapid Response Team on helicopter standby. Jeff they're heading West on the 80 to the airport"

"I know a short cut," he said.

"Sergeant scramble RRT and head for the airport. We have contact."

The black carrier pulled off the main road and entered the industrial estate next to the perimeter. Jeff stopped. Large hanger doors opened long enough to allow the vehicle entry and closed again.

"Sergeant it's time for the RRT to go in now," said Harriet.

Jeff looked at her and made to open the door.

"Just a minute where are you going?" she said. "Do you think for a minute we have the fire power to rescue Dashkevich? This is not what happens in real life you know that."

Jeff shrugged his shoulders. "Ok this is your call."

A helicopter descended and hovered thirty feet above the ground. The specially trained team abseiled to the ground panning out to take their positions. Three Simon breach grenades were launched destroying the door followed by shouts and a rapid assault by a dozen of the team firing as they entered. A massive fire fight ensued with periodic small explosions. Harriet looked at Jeff.

"Now do you believe me?"

"Why are you always so know it all, pain in the but, told you so, right? Can you not be wrong occasionally to give us mere mortals a chance?"

A Humvee emerged crashing through a corrugated wall and raced off. Jeff and Harriet gave chase. The road circled the airport to a dead end leading into a quarry. "This road doesn't go anywhere we've got them," said Jeff.

The Humvee disappeared down the track leading to the floor of the quarry three hundred feet below. Jeff stopped at the edge. There was a helicopter waiting with its blades turning.

"Do you want to go after them?" he asked.

"Let's see what we have in the trunk."

 They got out of the car and opened it. Two M4A1 assault rifles were encased inside designer boxes. "Have you used one of these before?" asked Jeff.

"What do you think?"

The Humvee had reached the helicopter and people were getting out running towards it.

"I don't see Dashkevich. Try and cripple the helicopter before it takes off."

Jeff loaded the assault rifle and took aim at the rotating blades. The men had reached the helicopter as it was beginning to take off. Jeff fired a short burst. Bits of propeller went flying spiralling the helicopter round and round until the tail hit a bank turning it on its side. The momentum of the few remaining spinning blades heaved the helicopter up in the air and it landed nose first with a huge explosion. Harriet and Jeff stood up on the edge of the quarry.

"Jeff, I said cripple it before it takes off." She took out her phone as they looked down at the smouldering lump of metal. "Hello... its Detective Sullivan, send ambulances to the airport quarry."

The got into the car and drove down into the quarry, stopping near the smoking helicopter. She checked the GPS signalled and it indicated one of the six charred bodies inside was Dashkevich. They left and made for the hanger. Inside an acrid smell of burning plastic and cordite filled the air.

"Are you guys' Ok, what's the count?" asked Jeff.

"We're clear. There are eight combatants dead one seriously injured.

"There are another six dead in the quarry. Can I see the injured man?" asked Harriet. They walked over to a corner of the hanger. Harriet looked at the man sitting on the ground leaning against a pile of pallets. She turned to Jeff and sighed. "let's get back." The peace was shattered as ambulances started arriving with lights and sirens blaring. "This is an almighty mess. Something seriously stinks. How did these guys know we were shipping Dashkevich out to a safe house?" Harriet kicked the tyre.

8

"No."

"What?"

"It's not necessary now we don't have to."

"Grainger what's happened to you? You gave your word."

"No you gave your word."

"You agreed."

"The circumstances have changed."

"Her grandmother is dying there's no one else." Grainger shuffled some papers and went to pick up the phone but Harriet's hand covered his.

"I have some time that I'm due I want to take off, maybe a week."

"What? in the middle of your first homicide?"

Grainger picked up a waste paper basket and threw it against a filing cabinet making Harriet jump. Everyone in the open plan office stopped what they were doing and looked towards the Sergeant's office.

Grainger stood up towering over Harriet. "Does this little girl that you've never met mean so much to you?"

"Yes…but it means a lot more to her."

He pointed at her with a stubby nicotine stained finger. "You…

you...," red in the face he let out his breath in one and paced around the room until he was calm then sat down. "Every so often someone comes along that sees things differently. There's a clarity of thought that's beyond just focus and concentration. It's a sign of a generational DNA hard-wired cop intellect," he pointed at her. "Don't think I'm referring to you because you're not even close yet." He got up and looked out through the glass door. "See all these guys, they're competent, dependable, loyal and they'll be doing the same job they're doing now until they retire. You did well today Sully, we have yet to identify who all these people are but a substantial number of them appear to be freelance mercenaries from Belarus. But, sometimes just sometimes you push me too far. I'll speak to the Captain but don't think for a minute I'm going soft. By the way the FBI wanted to know if you could be seconded to their team. I said no I need you here. Thought you might like to know that in case you heard it from someone else. Now if your head will fit through the door, get out of my office."

"Thanks Grainger I really appreciate that. There's something else..."

"...No."

"Grainger there's something I really do need to tell y..."

"...Out, get out."

Harriet started laughing much to his consternation. He got up and opened the door pushing her out then slammed the door behind her.

Ben was waiting. "Is everything Ok? I saw the waste paper basket bouncing around Grainger's office." Harriet rolled her eyes. "Have you had a chance to look at the results of the algorithm?" he asked.

"Let's go to my desk and run through it. I'll meet you there in a minute."

Jeff was typing away on the computer as she passed. "What are doing to Grainger you're going to get thrown off the force and then I'll have to answer to Nancy," he said.

She put a hand on his shoulder and whispered. "I tried telling the Chief about Dashkevich's notes and he wouldn't let me speak. Can you call on the Property and Evidence Bureau and pick up the Melissa Miscellaneous envelope and bring it up. I'm just about to go through some logarithms with Ben."

Harriet stopped at the coffee machine poured out two cups and went to her desk. She looked at Ben. "Hey how'd you get past my login?" He gave her a withering look and continued typing. "You're quite excited about this aren't you?" she said.

He giggled, "I'm trying to stay cool." He punched away at Harriet's keyboard. "Now these are all the cases that popped up. You're not going to believe it. I have found fifteen potential homicides. Eight of those worked for either one of the two companies under investigation, another three worked for Gerrard Associates the hedge fund managers, four had no direct connection with any of the companies...," he hesitated.

"...Why did they pop up?" asked Harriet.

"They were related to employees of both businesses. But...and this is the most interesting part..."

"...Speedy was the medical examiner in all of the cases," said Harriet interrupting.

Ben sat there with his mouth opening and closing like a goldfish. There was a light tap on the desk. Ben and Harriet turned to see Jeff standing there with an envelope.

"Ben you're magnificent, I'm going to ask HR to give you a rise. When you get a chance try and find out more about the victims, autopsy reports, who the case officers were, what were the circumstances, anything you can find out. Sit down Jeff, here," she handed him the coffee. "Ben's just found another fifteen potential victims."

Jeff handed her the envelope. She opened it and took out Dashkevich's envelope then hesitated looking at Jeff. Opening it she took out the two pages and unfolded them. She stared at them.

"Well?" asked Jeff.

"How's your Russian?" Harriet scanned the two pages into her computer and converted them using OCR to a Word document then translated them both online.

'Skillet mesh name commercial provisions in Belarus previous security exported to everywhere...'

This is not making any sense we'll have to get a Russian translator do you know anybody Ben, somebody trustworthy?"

"Yes, my brother." Ben copied and pasted the text into a secure encrypted email client and sent it. "Did I tell you he works for NSA's non-existent hacking team?"

Harriet had been thinking hard. "We have to draw up a plan of action here and I'm not talking about Homicide. There are some rotten apples in our barrel and we need to find them. Getting Dashkevich out of here was too easy it must have been Okayed by someone high up in the department. Who can we trust?"

Jeff drank some coffee. "Well the three of us obviously and the Sergeant and I've known the Captain a long time I can't believe he's bent. The DA is alright he's taken chances on cases he could have walked away from. The assistant DA? I don't know maybe, Bingham? Wouldn't trust him if my life depended on it." He took another sip.

Ben turned from the screen. "You've forgotten someone, Speedy."

9

"I'm running out of space. I don't know why they're here they've clearly all been shot," Said Dr Speed.

"Have you had a chance to examine the bodies?"

"Externally yes. Are they Russian, they're covered in Cyrillic tattoos and symbols."

"Have you got photographs?"

Speed went over to a computer, saw Harriet's tablet on Bluetooth and transferred the file.

"Have we been invaded by the Russians?" he asked.

"They're not from Russia." It occurred to Harriet that there was an element of forced casualness in his conversation that was uncharacteristic. She studied the photographs without replying.

"What do you know about tattoos Henry?"

"I would imagine they would hurt rather a lot."

"Oh um so, no conclusive evidence about Joe Simmons death then?"

"No, no evidence conclusive or otherwise."

"Thank you Henry."

Harriet pushed open the door of the gents' restroom with a loud bang and found Jeff using a urinal.

"I've been looking for you everywhere."

"Harriet for goodness sake…," he said turning his back on her.

"…It's important." She leaned against a line of basins watching.

"You can't come in here it's embarrassing."

"You haven't got anything I haven't seen."

A toilet flushed, the door opened and Ben came out. He shook his head. "I don't know. I'm not going to say a word. I give up with you two," he said washing his hands.

"Jeff I want you to invite Grainger to dinner tonight, say eight o'clock?" Jeff pulled a paper towel from the dispenser and wiped his hands.

"What? Sully! I have plans for tonight."

"Cancel them Ben and I are coming,"

"Am I?"

"We need a powwow at a venue that won't be noticed. Don't worry, I'll bring along some pizzas and beer. Please ask him and don't tell him why, don't take no for an answer, *capisce*?"

"I got a translation from my brother, haven't opened the attachment yet," said Ben.

"Print off four copies and take them along tonight. I have some interesting photographs of dead naked Belarusian ex secret servicemen with tattoos. Oh and bring along copies of the list of suspected homicides. Have you been able to get any more info on them?"

"Yes a little more."

The door opened and Jack from Vice came in looking puzzled. "Have you lot not got desks to go to? Sully you know this is the gents right, the female of the species is persona non grata."

"Don't you start with the Latin," she said.

It was getting dark. Harriet sat in the Humvee on the drive outside her home on 7th Avenue looking at her smartphone. She clicked on Home App and checked security, all seemed clear. She looked out of the window at her house. She liked the idea that all the houses on the Avenue were different. Hers was an old detached brick building that she bought for a song because it needed a lot of work. The owners had inherited it and wanted a quick sale. She was attracted to the four slated Dutch roof gable ends supported by square plain columns. A circular window just below the apex of the roof was balanced by two double glazed windows with fake sash astragals. Below, an attractive bay window dominated the frontage and next to it a modest grey front door with a glass panel. She grunted as she pushed open the stiff Humvee door and got out clutching her tablet closing the heavy door with a bang. She walked up the steps, unlocked the door with a key from the replaced beef-up security locks. The door creaked as it opened surprising her, she didn't remember it doing that. Perhaps it was the extra weight of the new laminated glass. Inside it was unnervingly quiet and the air was stale. She picked up some circulars and a note from the floor and walked into the kitchen putting down her tablet on the oak work top.

'Detective Sullivan,
We have changed all your locks with the latest state of the art secure locking system used by senior government department heads. The glass on all exterior doors have been laminated and are bullet proof. The lockable double glazed windows are now secure. More locks have been added to the upper windows on all sides. The access door from the attached garage has been replaced to add further security. Do not lose your keys otherwise someone will have to smash down a door for you to gain entry. We have made your house as protected as possible. You can feel secure in the knowledge that there is no access to your

home without a key. There is also a panic button in the kitchen and bedroom that will summon help when pressed.
Karl Bruhner
Security and Maintenance
SLCPD'

She looked at her watch showing 6.30pm, ordered pizzas and beers to be delivered to Jeff's address, called for a cab to pick her up at 7.30, went upstairs to her bedroom and into her bathroom turned on the hot water and undressed. The bruise had spread across several more ribs and turned green, yellow and blue. She got into the bath and lay back enjoying the warmth. The phone rang but she couldn't care less, for the next hour she was off duty. She thought about the images of two killers with guns raised checking each room and spending time in her office. It was a violation knowing strangers had managed to invade her privacy and yes it had shaken her sense of security but she would get over it in time. It was not like rape. She had interview many victims when she was seconded to vice it was not like rape. The ones who had chosen to enter her house were dead and although others might follow, she would be ready for them. Harriet knew an investigation into the Simmons murders would open a big can of worms but the FBI agent in conference room five that asked 'where is this taking us?' was smart, very smart. Who knows where it would lead, who knows who would be hurt in the process. It was a high risk high return game. Despite the hot water a shiver ran down her spine. She knew that someone somewhere was planning either an accident of some kind or maybe one of Peter's obscure tropical rain forest poisons nobody had ever heard of and then she would end up on a slab with Speedy Gonzalez standing over her holding a circular powered medical saw with a grin on his face.

'Natural causes Captain, can't find a single thing wrong with her. Healthy? She's the healthiest dead body I've ever seen, yes sir'.

The marble slab was very cold and she didn't like the way he was looking at her and where he was looking. She heard the electric saw turning, not loud just a single tone like a dentist's drill.

'I found an extraordinarily obscure poison and it's rather unusual because it paralysis the body giving the impression of death. The breathing is so shallow it's imperceptible. The muscles can't move, neither can the eyes.'

The saw whined louder.

'This is going to hurt quite a lot actually.'

Harriet woke up with a scream and sat up in the bath breathing heavily. She looked at her phone, it was 7.15.

"He's not here."

Harriet took out her phone and went through her address book, dialling. "Grainger are you on duty?"

"No, what the heck Sully."

"In that case get your but round here."

"What for, I value my off duty time."

"For several very good reasons that I'm not going to talk about on the phone."

"No Sullivan."

"Ok let me put it another way, your future as a cop is in the balance."

"Harriet, I don't know how you get away with it," said Jeff.

"Natural charm I guess. Nancy are you wearing a new shade of lipstick," Jeff rolled his eyes and handed Ben a cold beer.

"Nancy which plug did you want me to change in the kitchen? Can you show me." She put her cup to one side and got up, "excuse me Harry, family conference."

He closed the door. "This is rude," he kissed her.

"When Grainger arrives and we start talking about work can you make an excuse and leave us, just until we finish. It's very important."

"Of course, is that it," he nodded.

"No problem."

The doorbell rang. They both went to the door to greet Grainger. He was a little grumpy. "Hi Nancy, Jeff. Where's Detective Sullivan?"

"They're in the dining room please just go through, Grainger will you excuse me I have a little headache."

"Sully what's going on, what's all this stuff, are you setting up your own police department?"

"Sit down Grainger and take the weight off your scruples. There are three separate things you need to know about that are connected. Ben has written an algorithm that flags…"

"…What's an algorithm?" Grainger asked. Harriet looked at Ben.

"Basically algorithms are instructions to a computer to search data in a particular way. So I created an algorithm instructing my computer how to find data that I was looking for," he said checking his screen. "I searched hundreds of accidents, natural deaths, suicides and I came up with fifteen possible homicides."

"Are you saying that there are fifteen people in this city…"

"…State."

"…that have been murdered and their deaths disguised?"

"Yes."

"Sully why are you not presenting this to the department

collator."

"I just received it this afternoon and this is the main reason why I wanted you here. There is at least one person in the department that's working for the bad guys."

"Who?"

"Grainger before we get on to that let Ben finish."

"Of the fifteen 'suicides' three worked for Universal Defence and Development Contractors Corporation, and two worked for Bailey and Bailey International Commodities Broker Incorporated. The others were relatives of employees in both companies. The senior medical examiner in every autopsy was Dr Henry Speed."

"So what are you saying Ben?"

"I think they were rocking the boat. Listen, an accountant qualified in international tax laws, manager of human resources, international freighting manager, night security guard, junior company lawyer, cyber security technician, data analyst and company medic. These are all key jobs within the company. These are people who are intelligent enough to know that there's something going on that's not right."

There was silence while they allowed Grainger to absorb it all. Harriet put down her pizza.

"Apart from the Captain and the Chief, the only people I can trust in the department one hundred per cent are sitting round this table right now. But that's not all Grainger."

"I'm getting a headache."

"Have a beer. I persuaded Dashkevich to write down what he knew in case anything happened to him before we could get his daughter to the States. I promised I wouldn't open it unless he was dead or his little girl arrived safely. As you know I promised him no matter what, Katya would find a new life in America. He wrote it in Russian and we've just had it translated." Harriet handed over the papers to Grainger. As he read it, she explained. "As you can see Dashkevich has named the gangmaster that imports killers from Belarus but not just in Utah. There are lists of addresses, safe houses, arms stashes etc. He traffics these guys in almost every state in America it's like a franchise. He told me he knew about the corporate shenanigans but he was either exaggerating or he was using it as insurance in case I opened the envelope early. So there's nothing about the operation of the companies we're investigating."

"So you're saying the department is Swiss cheese what do you suggest we do?"

"I'm working on it. How are the FBI getting on with their investigation of these suspect companies," she asked.

"Haven't heard a thing but that's not unusual when it comes to them."

"As much as it pains me to say so, they should take over the killer trafficking business. Hand it all to Chief McLeod not Deputy Chief Bingham."

"Sully you're a cop, you don't understand office politics. I can't go over Bingham's head."

"Alright pass the file directly to the FBI, no questions. Grainger I want to go undercover, get me into Bailey and Bailey."

Grainger shook his head. "I can't give this directly to the FBI, I'd get skinned alive...Ok I'll give it to the Chief. What are you going to do? Have you forgotten you're on a hit list, are you going to wear a wig and glasses, come on. See me in to my office tomorrow and we'll try and work out a plan."

When he had gone Harriet remembered the photographs and pulled out her tablet. "Have you got a monitor Jeff?" He disappeared and came back with one, sat it on the table and plugged it into the mains. Harriet linked her tablet to it and the folder appeared on the screen with thumbnails."

"What's this?" he asked.

"These are the dead foot soldiers from Belarus."

"Why am I looking at muscle bound naked dead killers?" asked Ben.

"Don't you see it?" Ben and Jeff looked at each other. "The tattoos," she said.

Jeff took a swig of beer. "Ok they have body art along with soccer players, gymnasts and young girls, so?"

Harriet laughed and shook her head. "It must be getting late. This is not body art this a record of the things these individuals have done in the past. Haven't you read the Russian Tattoo Iconographer Vsevolod Yermolov's 'Russian Prison Tattoos Coded Meanings?" They looked blankly at her. "They're still trying to identify these guys so let's just number them one to eight. If you examine number one's lower back you can just make out a line of small skulls, there are eighteen. This denotes the number of hits, people he has murdered. Do you see these bluish blurred tattoos here, he got those in prison and judging by the number of threads in his spiders web, he was in prison for one, two, three, four, five, six, seven years. This tattoo of a playing card with the image of a sand hour-glass, he failed to pay a gambling debt. Number three has a tattoo of Vladimir Putin over his heart, that doesn't mean he loves Putin, he was hoping a firing squad wouldn't shoot at the image. Number five has had a forced tattoo removed from his forehead which could mean many things that were intended to mark him out for having done something particularly evil against the criminal class code. Now this is interesting, number seven has a crown tattooed on his shoulder blade. That would indicate he was a leader at some point in his life. I can't help but get the feeling that it won't be long before they replace these guys."

10

"Breaking news on Coast to Coast Network Television. CCN have received a statement from the FBI. In the early hours of this morning synchronized raids by the FBI across thirty-two States have apprehended sixty-seven illegal immigrants from Eastern Europe and a cache of weapons. Over to our crime correspondent Laura McNally."

"Details are emerging of the most audacious raids and widespread crackdown on organised crime for decades. It appears that all sixty-seven men detained are ex-military trained personnel who have been trafficked from Belarus by a gangmaster who is in hiding. It is unclear what the intended role of these mercenaries was in America but there is disquiet on Capitol Hill at the ease at which such a large number of gunmen entered the country undetected. CCN understands that a crisis meeting of the FBI, Homeland Security, NSA and CIA is taking place right now to attempt to plug this back door entry into the US. The President has ordered an inquiry into the security services asking the question, why did they not know about this? Laura McNally from Capitol Hill."

Harriet's phone rang. She finished pouring milk into her cereal bowl turned down the sound and picked up the phone.

"Hello? Hello Jeff"

"Have you seen the news?"

"Yes I was just watching it, half expecting some mention made of the SLCPD, that could have been awkward."

"It could have been very awkward. The gang boss escaped."

"How come they didn't get him what's his name?"

"Gleb Durchenko."

"Huh, do you think he was tipped off?"

"Almost certainly."

"I bet he's not the only one who escaped the net. Why does that not surprise me. Ok thanks Jeff I'll be in shortly. Harriet turned up the sound again.

"Senator we're getting unconfirmed reports that these men were brought into the US and employed as contract killers isn't that a bit scary?"

"I agree if that is the case it is extremely alarming. We need to know how these men got into the country so easily and until we do we can't be sure that there are not more on the way..."

The phone rang. Harriet switched off the sound and answered. "Hi Dad happy new year I meant to phone but I've been working since early on new year's day, how's Mom?

"She's fine honey and how are you enjoying your first murder case?"

"Enjoying? No enjoying is not a word that springs to mind but I get a great deal of satisfaction when we put someone away, how's Florida? It's freezing here."

"Sunshine state, says it all. Can't stand the cold any more."

"So have you been partying?"

"We've had a few friends round. Harriet I have some bad news, it's about my brother, uncle Larry. You didn't really know him all that well did you?"

"Not really. Why what's happened?"

"He had a really bad accident in his car. I'm afraid he didn't survive the crash.

"Oh Dad I'm so sorry."

"You did meet him by the way."

"Dad you have so many brothers and so does Mom I don't think I've met them all, when did I meet him?"

"He went to your graduation."

"My graduation? Well it's a bit of a blur, what happened to him?"

"His car left the road and rolled down a hillside when he was coming back from a skiing trip.

"Oh no that's awful."

"The funeral's tomorrow, Harrison Funeral Home in Ogden, Weber County.

"I'll find it. I'm sorry Dad, bye."

Harriet put down the phone and picked up her bowl of cereal. She watched the news bulletin with the sound turned off. A sadness enveloped her. Not for her personal loss but for the effect it would have on her father. Uncle Larry was younger than him. She really didn't know much about him other than he was a bit of a maverick. Family gossip hinted at his ownership of shares in a casino in out of state Reno, the nearest thing you can get to gambling in Utah is bingo. He also owned a string of race horses trained by well-known retired jockey Gerry Fitzsimons at his training center on the outskirts of Ogden City. Uncle Larry was a live-wire, goodness knows what else he was into and Harriet preferred not to know.

Harriet tapped on the Sergeant's door and popped her head in. He was on the phone. "Just a minute," he beckoned her in. "That'll never stick you need more, yeah, bye."

"Did you see the news?"

Grainger nodded. "There are a lot of smiling faces in the FBI right now thanks to you."

Have you thought any more about me going undercover?"

"Told you last night, I can't risk it Sully, you're too high ranking, but I admire your offer, the FBI was quite clear that they wanted to handle it. If necessary I might be able to place someone else from surveillance."

Harriet looked at him taking it all in. "I have to go to a funeral in Ogden tomorrow I might not be back until the afternoon is that Ok?"

"Sure, but try and get back ASAP. Grainger's phone rang."

Jeff wasn't at his desk so Harriet went down to see Ben.

"Hi, how are you getting on with Simmons tablet?"

Ben leaned back in his chair and rubbed his eyes. "There was no external memory card so it is wrapped in packs of silica gel drying out and that's going to take a couple of days. Normally I would de-solder the memory chip but I've deleted memory as a result in the past so if you are happy to wait, this is by far the most reliable method of retrieval."

"Fine with me what about the memory stick these guys plugged into my computer, what was on it?"

"There were lots of interesting tools." Ben brought up an image of a list of files and folders. "All made in Russia. This one is a brute force attacker and it's quite sophisticated. I reckon that if the guys had arrived five minutes later they would have been in and gone. If they had succeeded to get in, this one explores the contents of your hard drive, emails, documents, any interesting photographs you might have and it can encrypt it, locking you out. This one is a very sophisticated key logger undetectable by any antivirus software. It would be able to access any bank account credit card account, Ebay, Amazon. If they wanted they could enter your account change password details lock you out. This one takes control of your microphone and onboard camera so that they could hear and see even if you thought you were off line and this one sends a worm into your router to find and compromise any router connected devices."

"Like Home Smart. So they could see me walking around the house and they would even know how much milk I have in the fridge."

"Exactly. There is no end to the fun they could have with your computer. They could even turn off your blanket on a cold night if they felt mean."

Harriet left forensics and slowly walked upstairs deep in thought she didn't notice Officer Hardy pass her on the stairs. She stopped and turned looking down the lower flight of stairs.

"Joan?"

Officer Joan Hardy stopped and looked up. She turned and walked back up stairs. "Hello Detective Sullivan."

"Have you got a minute?"

Joan looked at her watch. "Yes."

Harriet led the way to her desk. "Take a seat." Joan sat down. Harriet studied her, making her a little uncomfortable. "You left Melissa Simmons."

"Yes."

Harriet waited as the tension grew.

"I asked her if she would like a cup of tea. She said no and had a whisky and water. She said she felt better and seemed to have recovered from the shock. She talked about her husband, she was very proud of him but she was worried that one day something would happen to him. She knew he had a lot of enemies but he was always very protective of her, made sure she knew nothing. It didn't protect her though did it? It was a pointless killing."

"How long did you stay with her?"

"Just over an hour."

"An hour!"

"I got a call from the duty Sergeant, he said there was a 10-50 six blocks away. So I left her. The traffic was heavy. It took me a bit of time to get there and when I arrived at the scene, there was nothing there. I radioed in and I was told to return to HQ. However I wanted to make sure Melissa was alright and I made my way back but the traffic hadn't improved and then I got another call, domestic disturbance so I never got back to her." Joan put her head down.

"Did she seem suicidal to you?"

"No not at all. You know deep down I think she knew that her husband was on borrowed time. He was addicted to the spectacular exclusives splashed across front pages. It was like a drug. She told me he had a conveyor belt of stories from germination to fruition almost continuously. She wasn't suicidal, there was an emptiness, a sadness and a feeling of inevitability."

"Can you do something for me? Find the duty Sergeant and ask him where the information came from about the non-existent accident."

"I did he said there was a 911, a passer-by calling on a mobile, didn't give his name, number withheld."

Can you go to control and ask them to email me the file of the incoming call. Don't reproach yourself Joan, you didn't know what was going to happen none of us did."

"Ben are you busy?"

"Man I'm always busy, I'm the most overworked employee in this building. When I go home my partner asks for ID just to make sure it's me."

"Very funny, could you do a cross reference on the times that Joe Simmons phone was in contact with someone in this building against the roster. There's a chance that over, what was it a month?"

"Seven weeks."

"Seven weeks, that it might just throw up someone who was on duty here consistently on each occasion."

"I've already done it."

"Why didn't you say?"

"Because I'm busy, you're not the only Detective that has a call on my services."

"Whoa, Ok Ben chill. What did you come up with?"

Ben's printer started whirring. "This is a list of all the personnel that was on duty at each of the times and dates when there was communication between Simmons and HQ. Believe me it wasn't easy pinning these names down out of four hundred and thirty-two staff."

Harriet took the page from the printer and looked at Ben. "This can't be right."

Ben shrugged, "I'm just the messenger. The methodology is text book. I even checked visitor and outside trade sign in books."

Harriet sat down staring at Ben. "What you are saying…"

"…I'm not saying anything Sully, that's what the data threw up."

"Yes but is it accurate?"

"Of course."

She looked at the seventeen names on the sheet, ten she didn't recognise, mostly visiting trades people four were familiar. Officer Jennifer Baxter who works on cold cases, Damien Shaw a civilian HR manager, Harry Bell logistics and Martin Wheeler a forensic accountant. The other four were all too familiar. Dr Henry Speed, Sergeant Grainger Stokes, Detective Jeffrey Blackwell and Deputy Chief Bingham.

"Where's Simmons tablet?"

"Right here in my safe."

"Did I ever tell you that you're a genius Ben?"

"Yes many times. You'll have to come up with something fresher more elevated. Perhaps…"

"…I'll think of something." Harriet slipped the A4 page inside the sleeve of her tablet. "Ok this is what we're going to do. I want you to buy online an identical tablet, put it into a bag with silica gel tape it up and lodge it with the Property and Evidence Bureau. But before you hand it over to the bureau duty clerk, I want you to paint the tablet and the outside of the bag with UV reactive powder. If this goes missing and let's face it things do go missing from there regularly, all we need is a black light. The clerk will be alright he always wears blue surgical gloves. This is strictly between you and me. I owe you."

"Big time."

Harriet went along the corridor to technical support. "Marian, hey how's it going?"

"Good thanks, you don't pop in here often."

"I know, there's a little job I was hoping you could help me on. Can you come with me and I'll show you." They took the stairs till they reached the corridor on the Homicide floor. "Do you see the panel of strip lights above the doors to the ladies and gents toilets? I'd like you to replace one of the strips with a UV light and here next to it a fake smoke detector Wi-Fi enabled camera and I'd like it done very much in confidence."

"Sure, I'll go and do it now. It shouldn't take five minutes."

"If anybody asks what you are doing…"

"…I've been working here for the past ten years and nobody has ever asked me what I'm doing."

Harriet left Marian and went back to her desk. An email icon was flashing. She clicked on it to see an attached audio file from control. She played the file just as Jeff walked over. It sounded like someone trying to disguise his voice.

"Hello there's been an accident at the junction of Fifth Street and Oak Street, some people are hurt."

"This is the hoax caller that pulled Joan away from Melissa."

"He was probably sitting outside her house making the call waiting for her to leave," said Jeff.

"Good point." She picked up the phone. "Hi can you see if Officer Joan Hardy is still in the building? and if she is ask her to call me…Sullivan."

"Hello there's been an accident at the junction of Fifth Street and Oak Street, some people are hurt."

Harriet played it again.

"Hello there's been an accident at the junction of Fifth Street and Oak Street, some people are hurt."

"Would you say that's an East European accent?" asked Harriet.

"No it's like somebody pretending to be."

The phone rang. "Oh Hi Joan when you left the Simmons house were there any cars parked outside maybe with somebody inside."

"I'm sorry I was in a hurry."

"Oh Ok, wait was your car-cam recording."

"Yes."

"Great can you send me a copy of that."

"Of course, right away."

"Thanks."

Harriet looked at Jeff. She was wondering if she should tell him that he was on the list. She looked away at her phone pretending to text. With only her and Ben knowing who was on the list, this could get awkward. Harriet's email pinged just as Ben arrived. It was a WAV video file from Joan Hardy. Harriet chose the rear camera and clicked on play. As the police car moved away from the Simmons house it was clear that there were only three vehicles parked in the street. Harriet paused the recording. She could see the number plates of two of them, the third was partially obscured. Harriet emailed the file to Jeff.

"Jeff can you check out these license plates and see what you can do with the third one, there may be a frame that shows it clearly, thanks." Jeff went back to his desk. "I hate this," she said to Ben. "It's really awkward." She was watching Jeff at his desk while she spoke. "I don't suspect him for a second but I can't tell him about this, not yet."

Ben sat down. "I'm just a very small but highly important cog in a giant Meccano set and I'm comfortable within my digital parameters. I don't have to guess or second guess or make judgement calls. There is an indelible info-fingerprint of everyone who has ever clicked a mouse out there forever, accessible and permanent. Do you want me to delve into Jeff's digital past?"

"No of course not. Tell me Ben if anyone with the authority asked you to do a check on me, would you?"

"Of course Sully why wouldn't I? What about Speedy and the Sergeant?"

"We have to be really careful Ben we can't be seen to be running internet checks on colleagues and that means we can't run any checks. Are you going for lunch?"

"No I think I'll grab something from the vending machine and get back downstairs."

Harriet watched Jeff approach her desk.

"I managed to trace all three plates. One belongs to a neighbour the second is an insurance company car pool vehicle and the third…," he paused for effect, "…is a hire care rented to a private investigator named Dennis Peace."

"Let's go and see him we'll grab something to eat on the way."

11

It was a small office in a tired looking red brick building above a laundrette with a flashing neon sign saying 'LAUNDERIT.' Climbing the linoleum clad stairs there was no sign of a receptionist or secretary. Harriet tapped on the glass door and entered.

Peace looked up surprised. "Is that security entry system still not working?" he asked, annoyed.

"Dennis Peace?" he nodded closing the windows on his computer. I'm Detective Sullivan and this is Detective Blackwell. Did you hire a car from Smart-fleet vehicle hire yesterday?

"No."

"Your name and address was given to the company and a credit card with your name was used."

"Damn." He brought up a search engine on his computer and logged on to a bank account. "Damn, damn, damn it." He picked up a phone and dialled. "Hello, can I speak to William it's urgent." He looked at them both drumming his desk with his fingers. "Bill, freeze my account, I've just checked its nearly three thousand dollars light. There are withdrawals and payments that have nothing to do with me...yes cancel my card and issue a new one." He put down the phone.

"Can you prove that you didn't hire this car."

"I've never heard of them. Go to their depot, they've bound to have a CCTV set up at their office."

Jeff and Harriet left the disgruntled PI and stood outside on the side-walk. "Go and check out Smart-fleet. Get a copy of the CCTV video if they have one and if they've got the car back impound it for forensics. I'll get a cab back to the office."

"Melissa Simmons killer stole the identity of a private investigator and hired a car using a cloned credit card and drivers' license. There is a call out for the car and we're hoping that there may be some DNA when we find it."

Stokes was sitting at his desk, listening to Harriet. He was tapping his teeth with a pencil. Harriet's phone rang.

"Excuse me Grainger. Yes…Ok, thanks, yes just come back to the office. There's been a report of a burnt out car under one of the arches below the interstate."

"What else have you got?" The Sergeant opened a folder on his desk.

"Well forensics thinks they're close to drying out Simmons tablet, it's lodged with the bureau. Any sign of the gangmaster."

"No nothing."

"Anything from FBI?"

"No."

"I don't like this one-way traffic Grainger it's not conducive to interdepartmental co-operation."

"Interdepartmental poppycock? Where did you get the idea that the FBI co-operates with anybody from. If you've got anything to give them, give it to them, don't expect anything back. Giving is not what they do, that's not the way they work. Look Sully you're a bright kid, who knows you might even become Chief one of these days if it's what you want but be under no illusion they think we are a bunch of bumbling Keystone hicks that don't know our ass from our elbow."

"As long as they keep on thinking that the more we're likely to surprise them," she said. Grainger looked at her puzzled and slightly troubled.

Harriet walked between the lines of desks until she reached Jeff's. "Hi."

"Hi."

"I'm going to knock off early and head up to Ogden. It's personal I don't want to use the Humvee."

"You can borrow mine."

"No thanks Jeff I don't mind getting the coach." Harriet sat on his desk and thought for a moment. "Do you have one of those throwaway cell phones? You know a dumb one that doesn't have all the bells and whistles?"

Jeff opened a drawer and took out a basic model. "This is a Nokia I stopped using a few years ago when I upgraded. There's no internet connection, is this what you want?"

"Perfect, you can get me on this number, just you. See you tomorrow afternoon." Harriet went over to her desk and put her smart phone into a drawer closing it.

Harriet relaxed leaning against the window of the coach remembering how fast everything went once she had made the decision to join the police. It didn't really seem that long ago.

"Police? Not the police," said Harriet's mother. She was small and round and cuddly, normally a relaxed jovial person with a ready sense of humour and an infectious laugh. But now she was serious and anxious.

"Mattie women do join the police force," said Donald.

Harriet was twenty-one then fresh out of college with her degree.

"I thought you were going to be a psychologist."

"Mum I got my degree in psychology but there are many application many different fields in psychology and how better to apply it than in the police force?"

"Which part of the police force do you want to work in?" asked her father.

"Wherever they will have me," she lied knowing full well that her ambition would always be to work in homicide. "I start the assessment next week to see if I meet the Peace Officer Standards and Training Council requirements, then I have to complete the basic police academy program. Then, I hope to be hired by a Sheriff's Office or Police department. Anyway I'd prefer to stay in the city and amongst other things there is a psychological examination."

That is how it began. Harriet passed the tests and was accepted for training at the POST Academy in Sandy, Utah. It was rigorous and tiring but hugely enjoyable. After basic training amongst other courses there was firearms training, emergency vehicle operations, canine training, defensive and physical fitness and finally curriculum development. After completing four months during both blocks of training she achieved her certification for law enforcement necessary to work in the state. She started with the State-wide Information & Analysis Center (SAIC) as an Intelligence Liaison Officer but was itching to move on and after a year transferred to state's cyber-unit acting on the intelligence received. She was then assigned to cold case investigations, gathering information using advanced 21st century DNA techniques before moving on to vice, going undercover to help get information to stop human trafficking. Then she applied to join homicide.

It was getting dark when Harriet's bus stopped at Ogden Transit Center in Wall Avenue.
Waiting for her was James, her brother. They embraced.

"Where's Mom and Dad?"

"Dad's a bit upset. He's having a pre-dinner drink and Mom is at home in Florida." He said as they walked with care over the icy snow to his car.

"What's this?"

"Do you like it Harry? It's a nineteen seventy-two Lancia Stratos?"

"James when are you going to grow up?"

"Never I hope, this is a chick magnet."

"Haven't you got a regular girlfriend yet?" she asked climbing awkwardly into it.

"Why buy a book when you can go to the library. What about you?"

"I'm not even a member of the library."

The engine roared into life attracting a few envious glances from guys and girls and took off with tyres squealing. Uncle Lawrence's house was the only one on an elevation looking down on Ogden. James pulled up to the front door and stopped. He jumped out and opened Harriet's door. The snow crunched underfoot as Harriet attempted to get out.

"Harriet," her father was waiting and gave her a big hug.

"Hi Dad, you Ok?"

"Sure, sure come on in."

The Blackwell's kitchen has just been refurbished after Nancy's pay rise. It had cherry wood cupboards and drawers with a faux marble worktop and in between pretend brick tiles. On the stove was an orange pumpkin shaped pot that had just been used to cook a chicken. Flanked by the kitchen and the small dining table was a coat and hat stand with an oval mirror. A card stuck to it said 'Happy New Year.' A modern square down light above the table illuminated Jeff and Nancy.

"Harriet's acting a bit strange."

"Strange? Towards you?" asked Nancy reaching forward to touch his hand.

Jeff stopped carving the chicken breast and poured a little wine for himself and grape juice for his wife. "No not strange, different like there's something between us. No not between us, like an invisible barrier, an issue, a problem, I can't explain it."

"Have you spoken to her about it."

"No I'd feel foolish if it was just in my imagination."

"Didn't think you were that sensitive."

"I'm not, that's the point."

"Ok, do you want me to speak to her?"

"Definitely not. You know, it's her first case and without going into detail it's a very complicated mess. Various government departments are involved and there's no flow of information. The result is nobody knows what's going on."

"Maybe that's what's bothering her."

"Yeah Maybe," said Jeff unconvinced. "Nancy I've got this bad feeling and I'm concerned about you."

She put down her fork and knife and studied him. He avoided her gaze. "Is it about this case?" he nodded, "go on."

"I think you should take a few days off...out of town somewhere."

Nancy stood up and ran to the kitchen sink where she was sick. She came over taking a tissue from a box on the worktop and came back to the table dabbing the edges of her mouth. She sat down and carried on eating. "Do you like Harry?"

"Nancy..."

She raised her eyebrows.

"...Of course I like Harriet," he said squirming in his seat.

"No, do you like her," Nancy smiled at Jeff's discomfort.

"I like you."

"You haven't been to Gloria and Chuck's ranch have you? It's just east of the Buckskin Mountains in Arizona. Last time I saw my sister it was at young Jennifer's christening. I think I would quite like to see them again would you mind if I paid them a visit?"

Jeff looked at her and smiled, reaching for her hand. "I more than like you. When did you realise that you're almost as intelligent as me?"

"Shucks honey, you'll make me blush," she said rolling her eyes in a fake country girl style.

12

"How long have I been your father?"

"Dad don't be silly, you mean how old am I? Can't you remember? I'm twenty-nine."

"Oh yes, isn't it sad that the only time families come together is when there's a marriage or funeral? They're all arriving tomorrow morning."

Donald Sullivan put his arm round her. They looked down on the twinkling lights of Ogden from the warmth of the conservatory. A passenger jet with its flashing beacon was making its final approach to Ogden-Hinckley Airport.

"I don't think it's sad. Any opportunity to come together is a good thing, right?"

"We used to be quite a close family."

"How's Mom?"

"She's disappointed she couldn't come, she has a problem with her breathing, still getting pains in her chest, won't go to the Doctor she doesn't want to know." He shook his head. "She still paints though her eyesight is not as good as it was. Don't make any difference, there's still a demand for her modernist portraits. Do you remember when she started painting Paiute children in the poorest parts of Cedar City? Ended up painting millionaires in Florida. She's got an exhibition next month in a fancy gallery in Miami, you should come she would be pleased."

"What about you?"

"There's a friend of mine who runs a wilderness experience in the Everglades travelling by canoe. He sets up camp with no tents just sleeping round an open fire, with a mosquito net of course and I've been organising through local community groups to try and encourage kids from disadvantaged backgrounds to experience nature. It can be life changing believe me I see a difference when they come back from a trip."

"No I meant here," she said tapping her heart.

"You know Harriet I've never felt better. I went for a check-up last month and saw Peter, he kept scratching his head, saying 'how come your still alive?' I never know if he's joking or not you can't tell with Peter."

"Who's all coming tomorrow?"

"Everybody. I'd like to think it's got nothing to do with Lawrence's wealth, but you know what families are like."

"I'm here for you Dad." He squeezed her shoulder. "I think I only met him once."

"Twice, he was also at your christening. You know there was something about the date you were born that affected him, he never explained."

"I'll be glad when this is over."

"I'm proud of you Harriet not because of the promotion to Detective but because I know that you're good at what you do but I worry about you, Homicide, really?"

"Could be worse I spent two years with the vice squad. Dad, I don't know if you're up to it but what happened to Uncle Lawrence?"

"Let's talk about it tomorrow."

The evening meal was simple and quick with very little said. It was as if Lawrence Sullivan's presence was being felt. Harriet decided to retire early and excused herself. Her room was large with numerous downlighters and a picture window that ran the length of one side with no blinds. Outside a snow clad hillside glistened below a star studded sky lit by a waning moon. Harriet changed into pyjamas and brushed her teeth when her phone rang.

"Hello Jeff."

"Hi, I thought Nancy should be out of the way, somewhere safe, especially now she's pregnant.

"Good, I think that's a very good idea. It's better she's out of town. I'm convinced somebody in the department is feeding information. Are you Ok you sound a bit strange?"

"Is there something going on I should know about, something you're not telling me?"

"Jeff...what do you mean is there something I'm not telling you? There are lots of things I don't tell you. Don't be paranoid I have to act on information coming in and go through procedure you know that but I have absolute faith in you."

"I feel I'm not in the loop."

"No, you're not...I can't discuss it with you, you just have to trust me."

"Are you sure you're Ok?"

"Yeah I'm Ok. I feel for Dad, he's a bit upset"

"When are you back?"

"Sometime after lunch around two-thirty. Get me as much as you can about these so called natural and accidental deaths. Tell the Sergeant I'm on it as soon as I get back, the chances are that the killers are either dead or in the can. Say high to Nancy. Oh Jeff, chill."

The walls and pillars of the panelled hall, one of four at the Crematorium were pale cream. Lines of comfortable red chairs faced a large window where the organist sat waiting. To the left lay the coffin. Donald Sullivan stood by the lectern in front of the organ nervously waiting for a last minute couple to sit down. He looked at the assembled gathering disappointed that only half the seating had been filled, took some notes from a breast pocket of his dark blue suit and placed them on the stand. Harriet sat on the front row and her thoughts and attention settled on the white casket resting on rollers flanked by flowers waiting to disappear behind two small red curtains. She wished she had made more of an effort to get to know her father's brothers and sisters. Maybe that's what her New Year's resolution should be.

"Lawrence Sullivan was an enigma," said Donald at the lectern. "He was kind, thoughtful and generous of spirit and substance yet he enjoyed his privacy. He was also some would say a non-conformist, I would call him a one off, unique. He was a very successful businessman though why he chose some of the businesses he worked in only he knows. I have very fond memories of Lawrence especially when we were young. He taught me how to get more bubble-gum out of the machine, how to make a bolas and then proceed to terrorize the neighbourhood. But most of all he showed me that there is nothing quite like the unconditional love of a brother. I think it would be fair to say that Lawrence never uttered a bad word about anyone and no one had a bad word to say about him. It's also fair to say that he wasn't particularly religious. However not many people knew that he recognised and supported Latter Day Saints humanitarian aid in countries affected by disasters around the world. The stricken people of Japan, Haiti, Samoa, Chile and the Philippines to mention a few who have been helped. The world, my world, our world is a sadder place without him but his memory will be with us always."

About half of those attending the service came back to the house after the Crematorium. The atmosphere was subdued. A familiar face appeared out of the crowd beaming at Harriet. She tilted her head looking sideways.

"I know you but I'm sorry I…"

"…Billy Brands, I'm still on the force, retire next month. You've done well Harriet."

"Thank you, of course I remember, how are you Mr Brands?"

"You don't want to hear about that, I'll be glad to hand in my badge."

"What happened to Uncle Lawrence?"

"You don't know?" she shook her head. "He was skiing at Powder Mountain Ski Resort, spent a week there and it happened on the way home…"

"…Billy it's time to go," said his wife was tugging his arm.

"Be with you in a minute. His car left the road and fell about five hundred feet, it broke up across the hillside."

Harriet watched as Billy's wife held on to his elbow. "Wait a second, has forensics checked the car?" she asked.

"No, there was no reason to, the traffic fatality unit did a routine procedural check as best they could and found nothing."

"Has the vehicle been brought in?"

"No and it won't be easy there's still a chunk of it dangling on the edge of a precipice. It's too far for heavy equipment. I suspect it'll just get left until it rusts away."

Harriet looked at her watch. When her father caught her arm. "This is Frank Calderwood, he's Lawrence's lawyer." They shook hands.

"Ms Sullivan I saw you looking at your watch are you about to leave?"

"Yes I have pressing work to do."

"Oh, would you care to stay on for an hour or so?"

"Why?"

"It's important."

Harriet took out her phone and walked to the window looking out to see Billy Brands and his wife leaving. "Jeff I may have another victim to add to the others."

"Really, who?"

"My uncle, Lawrence Sullivan."

"What's his connection to the investigation?"

"Me."

"What happened?"

"He supposedly drove his car off a cliff."

"Sully I think that's very unlikely. Apart from you there is no connection. It doesn't make any sense.

"Maybe I'm wrong, I don't know. I'm going up there to have a look."

"Take care Sully."

"Ok, bye." Harriet went out and down the steps of the house flagging down the car that was leaving. "Billy could you take me up to the scene of the accident?"

"Sorry Harriet I'm on the duty roster manning the desk. Hold on." He picked up his phone. "Hi Lucy is anyone kicking their heels."

"Yes Serge, Veronica."

"Good can you ask her to come out to the Sullivan household there's a Detective Sullivan that requires some assistance, thanks Lucy. Ok Harriet it was nice seeing you again after all these years Harriet, bye."

She went back into the house and saw her father beckoning. She followed him into Uncle Lawrence's office where several people were already waiting. Harriet sat down on a three seater leather sofa next to her father.

"Since you are all here in one place I thought it was best just to get the reading of the will over with if that's Ok with everyone." He opened an envelope and pulled out the will. "We'll skip the legal niceties and get straight to it."

'To my beloved brother Donald who has everything he could possibly need except perhaps a decent set of false teeth, I bequeath my very precious 1937 Lagonda drop-head coupé convertible. Take care of it Donald. To the rest of my brothers, sisters, nephews and nieces with exception of Harriet I bequeath one million dollars divided equally between them. To Pauline my housekeeper I bequeath the cottage she presently lives in. To LDS I bequeath my shares in the Golden Jackpot Casino in Reno, make of that what you will'

There was a murmur in the room accompanied with smiles. Harriet looked at her watch for the third time.

"Finally I leave the residue of my estate namely Sullivan House the grounds and contents thereof, fifteen gun stores in Salt Lake City, $5 million dollars in government bonds and securities, six racehorses at the stables in Ogden and the apartment in Salt Lake City to Harriet Constance Sullivan."

There was a gasp. All eyes went to Harriet who stood up in shock with her mouth open. She looked at her father's bemused smile and back to Frank Calderwood. "I don't understand."

Calderwood handed her an envelope. She looked at her name and sat down almost landing on her fathers' knee. There was a knock at the door. It opened and the face of a young policewoman peered into the room.

"Am I interrupting?"

"No I think we're done."

"Detective Sullivan?"

"Yes Veronica I'll be out in a minute. Dad can I speak to you." Everyone stood up and filed out. She shook hands with Calderwood. "Thanks, it's a bit of a shock, what is the date on the will."
Calderwood looked at it "6ᵗʰ August 1988 with six amendments presumably reflecting his latest acquisitions."

"That's the day after I was born. This is going to sound a little bit strange Mr Calderwood...I don't quite know how to put it...has your office ever been broken into?"

Calderwood looked startled. "Yes twice, how could you possibly know that? The first time was about twelve years ago. They found out who it was and he was sentenced to seven years, Died after four in prison when he got involved in a fight. The second time was a week ago nothing was taken. We reported it but since there was no loss the police stopped looking. How *did* you know that?"

"Just a shot in the dark." Calderwood shook hands and left. "Dad I'm going up to where the accident happened with Veronica just to see for myself and then I'll go straight into town and catch the coach."

"You'll need boots have a look in the hall cupboard. Why don't you take a break sometime and come to Florida."

"I will."

"You know you don't have to work anymore. You could invest the money and have a tidy little income. Travel the world, meet somebody nice, do things ordinary people do."

"Working in homicide was never about the money Dad. There's a lot of bad people out there and they're winning." She kissed him on the cheek.

13

A fresh fall of snow covered the road as the white Ford Crown Victoria patrol car made steady progress uphill only occasionally losing grip.

"We're getting the new special-edition Ford Mustang patrol car soon, at least that's what we've been promised," said Veronica with a grin.

Harriet was looking at the steep drop on her side. She really did not want the death of her uncle to be another murder.

"What's it like in homicide?"

"Frantic almost all of the time. What do you do Veronica?"

"Traffic, I don't mind. We could do with you here though there's a lot of bad stuff going on in Ogden. I don't know if we're winning. There were only four murders last year but that's a testament to the quality of our surgeons. There were 298 violent crimes a couple of years ago shame we don't have the latest statistics. Yes Ma'am I'm happy driving my little car making sure nobody breaks the speed limit or jumps a red light. Do you mind my asking what it is you're looking for?"

"Just want to be sure it's an accident Veronica, that's all."

They pulled into a lay-by and stopped. Veronica got out as Harriet put on her boots and gloves. The trunk opened revealing a bulletproof vest, a shotgun, first aid kit, some medical emergency equipment and a thick jacket which Veronica put on.

They stood at the edge of the road looking down.

"It's going to be a bit of a scramble, can you see it, it's covered in snow." Harriet shook her head.

They started the descent stumbling on hidden rocks and slippery grass until they reached the burnt out vehicle. It was resting on its passengers' side with the front dangling precariously over the edge of a sheer drop. The heat of the fire had shattered all the windows. The drivers' door had been removed to allow access and the empty trunk had been left open. Harriet began brushing the snow off the car until she was satisfied she had a clear view of it all then she began taking pictures with her phone carefully covering all the angles of the wreck. She shook her head. It would be almost impossible to make anything out of this. Almost every panel had a scrape or a dent most likely due to tumbling over and over as it went downhill.

"Thanks Veronica I really appreciate you taking me up here, I really do."

"You're very welcome. If you're done, let's go."

Harriet email the photographs to Jeff from Ogden Police Department and caught the bus to SLC.

There was no sign of Jeff when Harriet went into the office. She fired up her computer and checked her emails the last one reading, 'come to my office when you get back,' from the Sergeant. Harriet suddenly felt weary. It still hadn't sunk in that she was a millionaire. She got up and left in search of a coffee.

"I'll have one too, you owe me." Harriet turned to see Jeff smiling. She handed him her coffee and poured out another. "Those pictures you sent, there was one that was very interesting." He took from behind his back a large printed blow-up of the rear drivers' side panel. "This panel is showing what's left of the pale yellow paint. However just here you can see very faint parallel scratches of green."

"Hold it, come with me." They entered the Sergeant's office after knocking.

"You're back, good. I've put in a request to the FBI for an update."

"Grainger, I want you to hear what Jeff has to say."

"These are photographs of Harriet's uncle's vehicle that went down a mountainside killing him. This one shows the smearing of green paint indicating a collision. Now the guys downstairs say that this car was hit at exactly the spot the driver was bound to lose control of the steering. It's classic police training on stopping a terrorist or a dangerous suspect who's driving a vehicle. Find a green car with yellow paint on the front passenger side panel and you've got the murderer."

"My uncle *was* murdered," said Harriet. "His lawyer's office was broken into a week ago and nothing was stolen. He kept a copy of Uncle Larry's will in his safe. Whoever killed him knew before… Oh my God," Harriet sat down, white as a sheet. "They're trying to buy me off with Uncle Larry's money, that's sick."

"You're not making any sense Sully."

"He left me five million dollars." Harriet walked out of the office.

Grainger gestured to Jeff. "Make sure she's alright."

Harriet sat down at her desk and remembering the envelope that Calderwood had given her, opened it.

'My dearest Harriet,
The terms of my bequest will come as a surprise to you, I know. And although it may seem as if I have been a distant relative on the horizon, I have followed your development with great interest and now you have been promoted to a homicide Detective, I'm very proud of you.

Nobody knows what I'm going to tell you now. When I was working in Reno all these years ago, I met Lorraine and we got married. It was a quickie marriage but it was sincere and truthful and we loved each other nevertheless. In time Lorraine became pregnant and I looked forward to breaking the news to the family. Four months into the pregnancy there was a complication. She was rushed to hospital and I lost them both. I called your father to tell him and he said that you had just been born. I didn't want to spoil his joy so I kept quiet. I called the hospital to speak to your mother and they told me the exact time of your birth. It was seconds after losing Lorraine and the baby. Because of that I have always felt a closeness to you. In death there is life and in life there is death. You gave me hope for the future and for that I am eternally grateful.
Your loving Uncle,
Lawrence.'

Harriet started crying. She'd had a roller coaster of a day. She had been left all this money, discovered her uncle had been murdered and now this letter. Her head was resting on her folded arms on the desk. She felt a hand on her shoulder and lifted her head to see Jeff standing there looking puzzled. She wiped the tears away stood up and hugged him when Ben walked in.

The look he gave them was one of resignation. He had done his best to no avail and just resigned to the inevitable and shook his head.

"Harriet had some really good and also some bad news," Jeff explained unconvincingly.

Harriet's phone rang. "Hello...," she put the phone down. "It's the Chief, let's go."

"Take a seat Harriet, Jeff." It was the first time the Chief had called them by the first names. "I've had a note from the FBI they want to pass on their appreciation at the good work the two of you have done. A large number of contract killers across America have been caught or killed because of you two and I would like to add my congratulations and thanks as well. If it hadn't been for you a great many more people would have been murdered. We're still looking for the gang master but we'll get him before he can set up another network. Now…do you have a problem with Andy Bingham?"

The question was like a bolt out of the blue catching Harriet and Jeff off guard. "Why do you say that Chief."

He played with a pen on his desk while studying Harriet without replying. "Because Sergeant Stokes came directly to me with your information."

"Sir, we know that someone in the building is feeding information outside. We have done a correlation between the calls logged on Joe Simmons phone against the duty roster. Deputy Chief is one of the names on the list."

"And the others?"

Harriet took her tablet off standby. "There were seventeen names on the list. Thirteen were either casual trades or maintenance etc. including staff that would have had absolutely no interest in live investigations."

"That leaves four," he said.

"Dr Henry Speed, Sergeant Stokes, Deputy Chief Andy Bingham…," Harriet hesitated and glanced at Jeff.

"…And?" Harriet put the tablet on the desk facing the Chief. He looked at it without the flicker of emotion. Jeff looked sideways at Harriet who avoided his gaze.

"All this means is that these people were in the building when calls were made to and from Simmons, correct?"

"Yes sir. I believe that someone tipped off the gangmaster from somewhere in the building. Chief I also have a list of potential murder victims disguised as suicides and accident, and natural causes that had close links to the companies under investigation or links to relatives of employees. There is a network of corporate bosses who are employing mafia style killings in disguise."

"How many victims are we talking about?"

"Sixteen. Sir I would like permission to talk to some of the relatives of those who have died."

"Give me one good reason why we shouldn't hand it over to the FBI who are investigating these companies anyway."

"It does not bode well when a Hick homicide department is way ahead of them."

"We need to clear something up first, Jeff your name is on the list what do you have to say?"

"I suspected it might have been. The list is not conclusive. Patrol officers are coming and going all the time without clocking. I guess I just have to be trusted…or not."

"Harriet?"

"There is nobody in this building I would trust more than Jeff."

"Ok that's settled. Both of you have my unofficial permission. Don't upset anybody, keep a low profile, every inquiry is routine, report directly to me and do not I repeat do not approach any corporate bosses. If it all pans out smelling of roses both of you could be in line for promotion, if it all goes pear shaped you're on your own. Now get out there and get some work done."

They walked downstairs engrossed with their own thoughts and turned left into homicide. Grainger was standing at the open door of his office with his hands on his hips. Harriet stopped as Jeff reached his desk. "Promotion eh," he mused.

"Nah not a chance, do you think I'm going to lose a good partner without a fight?"

Harriet walked over to Grainger who turned and went into his office. "I sent those photographs to Ogden," he said. "They've taken scrapings of the hit and run paint and they've identified the vehicle through the exact colour match. It's a brand new 2016 Chevrolet Tahoe. Where were you just now?"

"Green Chevrolet Tahoe? That's the same one that went into the back of my car."

"Where were you just now?"

"The Chief wanted to see us. He was looking for an update."

"He was asking you for an update?"

"Yeah."

"The Chief was asking you for an update? Any communication with anybody outside of this department goes through me. Update?" He waved her away.

Harriet walked through the main office. "Jeff can you check Chrysler dealerships in Utah for a 2016 pale green Tahoe. The same person that tried to push me into a line of traffic killed my Uncle. This is getting very personal."

The modern apartment block in a nice part of the city was on three floors. Harriet rang the first floor doorbell and waited for the door to open.

"Mrs Irving?"

Monica Irving stood with the door ajar, peering out over her reading glasses. Her clothes hanging loose told Harriet she had recently lost weight. She wanted to give her a hug.

"I'm Detective Sullivan from SLCPD can I come in I'd like to talk to you about your son Jackson if that's Ok."

"Come in." Mrs Irving stood back allowing Harriet to enter.

"Who is it Mom?" Harriet guessed this was Jackson's brother Brian.

She led Harriet into the spacious open plan dining/living room. "This is Detective Sullivan, Brian."

An angry young man stood by the kitchen door holding a dish cloth. "What do you want? We're just getting over his death and now you show up. We need closure now not more cops."

Mrs Irving gestured to a white leather sofa next to an expansive wall length window. "Have a seat um..."

"...Harriet. I can understand how you both feel and I don't want to intrude. There are one or two questions that I hope will give you both closure. I can come back if this is an awkward time, I don't want to cause any more distress."

Brian seemed to be holding back his anger while slumping down on another identical sofa. Mrs Irving ignored him and looked at Harriet. "Would you like some tea?"

"Thank you."

She disappeared into the kitchen.

"What do you think you're doing? Jackson's dead and that's an end to it. What are you hoping to achieve, he committed suicide jumping off an insurance building, why are you here? Mom's not well this whole thing has taken its toll, I'm asking you to leave."

"Where do you work Brian?"

"Bailey and Bailey," said Mrs Irving carrying a tray and putting it down on the coffee table. She looked at Harriet, "and Brian's twin brother Jackson worked for Universal Defence and Development

Contractors Corporation. It was always hush hush he never talked about what he worked on."

"Just a little milk please. Did your son have any problems, anything at all, money, health, girlfriends?"

"Health? Oh you mean because he was gay, no. He had absolutely no problems. There was no suicide note and no reason for him to kill himself. He had lots of friends thank goodness we live in the 21st Century," she sighed. "It was a terrible shock."

"Brian have you ever been threatened?"

The question caught him off guard and he leant forward with his mouth open staring at her.
"Within the company that you work for?" Harriet picked up a cup and sipped the tea without taking her eyes off him.

"No of course not."

Harriet wasn't convinced. She took a card out of her pocket. "Mrs Irving I don't believe it was suicide, I think he was pushed. I know this has come as a shock, this is my card please call me when you feel able to. Brian I'm trying to stop this sort of thing happening again. Jackson is not alone there are others and there will be more."

Harriet had just got behind the wheel of her car outside the Irving house when her phone rang. "Yes Jeff."

"There were three Tahoe's of that colour."

"Good work, I'm on my way in."

The traffic was getting heavier as she negotiated the lanes on the free-way and then she saw a Chrysler Tahoe in an outer lane following. She turned off at the next exit followed by the Tahoe then a left and it was still there in her mirror. She dialled 911.

"Detective Sullivan. I'm travelling South on Seventh being followed by a suspicious vehicle a green Chrysler Tahoe, request stop and search, suspects may be armed and extremely dangerous. I'm leaving this channel open."

Harriet stopped on the red. The Tahoe was in the next lane one vehicle behind. She clicked open the glove compartment and took out a Ruger LCP and slid it under her bag on the passenger seat then ensured all the doors bar hers were locked. Keeping an eye on the mirror she hadn't noticed the lights and was reminded by the car behind. She turned right into a quieter street followed by the Tahoe that who had changed lanes. She was avoiding a firefight on the main drag. A patrol car emerged from a side street behind them with lights flashing and siren sounding. Two more police cars were coming up behind and then the Tahoe took off. Three patrol cars closed off the street ahead and now she could see the driver and passenger as they came along side. The passenger was pointing a gun at Harriet. She heard a couple of shots as she braked turning the steering wheel in the direction of the Tahoe. It slewed to the right and flipped landing on the roof. Harriet stopped the car and watched. There was no need for bravado, there were plenty of cops to mop up the mess. An ambulance arrived as the two men were taken out of the car. One was clearly dead the other badly injured. Harriet got out and walked over to the upturned vehicle. She looked at the panel that would have made contact with her Uncle's car but there was no sign of any damage. She ran her fingers along the paintwork and felt faint ripples underneath. She took out her phone.

"Hi Jeff don't bother trying to find the Tahoe, it found me. I took them out with the Humvee, barely a scratch on it. When they bring the Tahoe in ask forensics to x-ray the front nearside panel I think there's been a respray job."

14

"Bring me up to date Jeff." Harriet was peering at the computer screen on her desk.

"It's not looking good for the survivor of the crash, serious head injuries. Hold on, yeah…Ok thanks. That was forensics, the car had been resprayed hiding evidence of a previous crash with minute traces of yellow paint matching that of your Uncle's car. There was no ID found on either men and…"

"…The car had been purchased using a stolen identity and credit card."

"Another dead end. Interpol are checking their facial, fingerprint and DNA records to see if there's a match and nothing so far."

"I went to see number one on the list Mrs Irving. Jackson's brother knows something. Let's divide the rest. Can you organise Officers Barry and Hardy, I'll take two, three and four. Let's have a meeting last thing tomorrow here." Harriet looked at her watch. It was getting late and she was tired. She picked up her phone and dialled. "Dad, I have some bad news…"

A wave of depression settled over her as she put on the handbrake switched off the engine and lights and got out of the car. She looked up and down the street but it was all quiet as usual, climbed up the steps and opened the front door. She picked up the mail lying on the mat and emptied the delivery box of groceries closing the door. There was an unwelcome quietness in the house she hadn't noticed before, maybe it was just the way she was feeling. She took out a non-alcoholic beer and a ready-made meal of Chicken Tikka with rice and put it in the micro-wave setting the timer for fifteen minutes. She switched on the television just as the microwave pinged, opened it, took out the steaming chicken and sat down.

"Deputy Chief Bingham what is the latest on the explosion?"

Harriet stopped eating and stared at the TV. The snow was blowing in his face forcing him to wipe his glasses with his hand and turning his coat white.

"The blast took out almost the whole floor of the Property and Evidence Bureau, there's very little remaining. It seems like the explosion was caused by a number of liquid gas canisters being held as evidence. There must have been a leak. It is very lucky that it happened during a shift change when the early shift had left and the next shift hadn't arrived otherwise there would have been no survivors."

Somehow Harriet wasn't surprised. She ate her chicken slowly. She had a bad feeling that the evidence bureau wasn't secure.

"What will happen to the cases coming up that required the evidence held in the bureau?"

"Sadly without the evidence they will not come to trial."

Harriet's phone rang, she turned down the sound.

"Have you seen the news?"

"Yes looking at it now Ben. By the way I'll get maintenance to check the camera tomorrow. What did you think of Bingham's performance, hard to tell if he was sweating or if it was the snow. Sorry Ben I'll have to ring off I need to talk to Jeff…thanks." Harriet carried on eating her meal and took a swig of the beer when the phone rang again.

"Hi Jeff, I've just spoken to Ben."

"What about the Simmons evidence?"

"I don't want to talk about it over the phone."

"Are you going in?"

"No, nobody died, that's someone else's baby, See you in the morning."

Harriet had a restless night thinking about everything that had happened. One thing was becoming apparent they were beginning to get desperate and with desperation comes carelessness.

"Did Esther leave a note?"

"You mean a suicide note, yes. It's on her laptop."

"It wasn't in her case file."

"No, nobody asked, Harriet left wondering how Sven Soderberg was taking the idea that his daughter had been murdered, he didn't seem interested."

"Can I see it?"

Sven Soderberg rose from his chair, opened a mahogany roll top bureau and took out the laptop. He opened it and found the note. "She never used a password, I don't know why," he said handing it to Harriet.

'Dad,
My life has become meaningless. I have no real friends. Even work seems to be getting on top of me I hate it. Nobody likes me. There's somebody trolling me on twitter and won't leave me alone. I hope you will understand.

Love you
Esther
X'

"Mr Soderberg I've seen a few suicide notes and their heart wrenching, this hardly qualifies. There is no viable reason for her to take her own life based on that note. It says on the file that she took an overdose, what was it she took?"

"They said it was barbiturates, I don't know where she would have got them she wasn't on medication. I looked at the bottle, it's a prescriptive drug but she didn't get it from her Doctor."

"Mr Soderberg I don't know how you will feel about this. But I think it is only fair to tell you that I have been re-examining sudden deaths in the state and there is a possibility that I cannot rule out just yet that your daughter was murdered. Would you mind if our forensics examined the laptop?" he nodded. "The terminology, the words and the sentence lengths, would you say that the grammar in the note was recognizably hers?"

"Not really. Why on earth would anyone want to murder Esther?"

"That's what I want to find out. Thank you Mr Soderberg, I'm very sorry for your loss."

Harriet left wondering how Mr Soderberg was coping with notion the his daughter had been murdered. She reached the car and the keys slipped out of her cold fingers landing in the snow. Another storm was coming through and the flakes were getting bigger. She found the keys blew on her fingers and opened the door. She sat behind the wheel and closed it. There was a limit to the sadness of others she could absorb but she was frightened of becoming emotionally calloused. Callousness and cynicism was rife in Homicide, understandably employed as a defensive shield. It must be so for all emergency front-line services. But, amazingly ambulance paramedics she knew who had seen every conceivable human distress and trauma there is, still remained caring. Soderberg was the last of her four sudden deaths, time to head back to the office. She switched on radio KZHT. An Al Cappella rendition of 'Silent Night' by Vocal Point began slowly, filling the car and the void. She drove on negotiating the traffic on automatic bathing in the beauty of the harmony and in the belief that life wasn't all about death.

"Marian did anything show up on the hidden camera?"

"Sorry, not a thing."

"Ok just wrap it, thanks." Grainger came over to Harriet's desk and sat down. He folded his arms and looked at her. She shrugged and swivelled her chair round to face him.

"What a mess. Where are we with all of this now?" he asked.

"I have a meeting later on this afternoon. There is a potential fifteen murders passed off as sudden deaths in this State not including my uncle and the Simmons."

"Did you have anything in the evidence bureau?"

"Yes."

"Shoot! What?"

"Grainger..."

"...We're compiling a list from memory of what was destroyed."

"What do you think happened to the store?" she asked.

"Bottles of liquid gas exploded."

"How?"

"I don't know, the arson squad are examining what's left now."

"It was deliberate," she said. "The timing ensured there were no casualties, and the motive was to destroy potentially damaging evidence."

"What did you have in there?"

"A tablet wrapped in silica gel."

"Simmons!" It wasn't a question so Harriet didn't answer. "So that's us back to square one. Are you any closer to knowing who the mole is?"

Harriet shook her head. "However," she smiled pausing for dramatic effect, "the tablet that was blown up was a decoy we have the real tablet in a safe place. I set a trap with the fake tablet but the explosion got there first. Maybe the mole spotted it. Grainger I'm going to ask you something which you are not going to like and you'll probably be offended. Apart from two or three people, Present company exempted I don't know who to trust in this department."

He sat down reached for a packet of cigarettes in his pocket and put one in his mouth. Harriet had often seen him with an unlit cigarette. "That doesn't offend me."

"I want to be able to operate alone...with my partner. That means no updates. Nothing passed on to the FBI, CIA, Homeland Security, Assistant DA..."

"...Or me?"

Harriet nodded. "Nothing personal. There are too many things going wrong. Where I can, I will update you on non-sensitive information."

"Ok let me give you an insight into my position on this. I'm supposed to know what everybody is doing at any given moment in time, why? because I'm responsible for every single thing that happens in my department and to stop you guys fouling up. If you foul up I foul up, get it. The question is can I trust you not to foul up and that includes getting in FBI's way and here you are asking me to give you carte blanche?"

"No I'm not, you'll just have to trust me Grainger every move I make has been shadowed and pre-empted by someone in this building. This is the only way we can crack this, you know that. There is no question that I will operate outside normal policing practice."

Grainger shook his head. "You have to report to someone."

"Alright who?"

"Me. I want a daily update and guess what you're just going to have to trust me. And there's something else. If I thought for one minute this was just an attempt to hog the limelight you'd be back on traffic."

"Grainger I've just inherited a fortune. I could walk out of this office and live happy ever after. I'm here because I want to do something worthwhile with my life."

Grainger got up and turned stabbing a finger at her. "I said if...if." Flecks of white spittle stuck to the corners of his mouth.

"That's not an answer."

"Would it make any difference?"

"Yes. Who gets to know after you?"

"I'll keep a lid on your investigation as long as I can. It won't be easy I get emails all the time from the Chief. He gets emails from the Mayor. Does that answer your question?" he said walking off.

Harriet went over to Jeff's desk. "How are you getting on with the sudden deaths?"

"It's all beginning to piece together, there's definitely a pattern emerging."

"Ok I'll check with the others, I'd like to bring the meeting forward, two o'clock briefing room three." She went back to her desk and dialled a number. "Detective Barry can you make two o'clock...briefing room three and can you check with Joan Hardy to see if she can make it thanks." She dialled again. "Ben are you busy right now, forget I asked that can I come in by?"

"Sure, why not?"

She started searching in a desk drawer when she was aware of someone standing next to her. She looked up to see a tall dark haired clean shaven man wearing spectacles and a bemused smile leaning against her desk with his arms folded. "How did you get in here?" she said surprised.

"It was probably a combination of my natural charm and a lie. I said you were expecting me."

"They should have called."

"You're line was engaged, how are you Harriet?"

She sighed, "the security in this place is terrible..."

"...I've missed you."

"You've missed me," she said. "Eliot Mitchell, you take a six month commission from the New York Times to write about Interpol's campaign against human trafficking across Europe and then you just walk into the office saying you've missed me. I can't deal with this part time girlfriend thing...and...and your timing is bad."

"Let's have lunch we have lots to talk about. I'll take you somewhere smart."

Harriet looked at him. He hadn't lost the spark that had attracted her to him but why did he have to be so cock sure about everything?

"I haven't got time for smart I really am very busy on a big case." She looked at her watch. "Mitch I have to go to forensics, I'll meet you in half an hour at Jan's Diner across the road."

15

Ben sent a Rexene swivel chair spiralling across the room and screamed just as Harriet walked in. He stretched out both arms sleeves rolled up palms down and breathed in deeply with his eyes closed glasses perched at the end of his nose. Pulling over the chair he sat down in front of a monitor waving at Harriet. "Somebody's trying to get in. This is not a pimply nosed geek doing it for kicks its serious shit. I haven't seen anything like it since the Stuxnet worm. It looks like a morphed variation of Duqu 2. This is not the North Koreans it's not East European Mafia. It's not China or Russia." He looked at Harriet. "This is home grown and somebody here in the good old US of A is targeting the SLCPD. I've checked on the forensics IT blogs and guess what? nobody else is being targeted."

"Has it done any damage?"

"Not yet it hasn't come up against my anti-mal architecture before but it keeps probing. My system is based on the maze principle where incoming have to 'handshake' there way through the maze. The path changes every millisecond so if it takes the wrong path or if the handshake is incorrect or if the journey through the maze is not completed in time, it fails setting off an alert. This particular attack keeps probing. Excuse me Harriet." Ben picked up a phone. "Chief, have you been watching."

"Yes, how bad is it?"

"It doesn't get any more serious."

"What should we do?"

"I recommend a complete server shutdown, isolate department servers and guide this sneaky little worm into a trap...Ok?" Harriet turned towards the door. "Sully I can't make the meeting but I've emailed stuff you'll find interesting oh and by the way I had a sneaky peaky at some emails from the two corporate CEO's. They're switched on to any potential hacker like me so the traffic all seems ridiculously banal. They must have an encrypted secure email client. When I get on top of this I'll do more digging."

Jan's Diner was almost empty. Jan watched Mitchell come in and sit down. "Hello stranger." She wasn't smiling as she spoke pouring out Mitch's coffee. "Back from your travels?"

"For now, I'm getting a little tired of it at the moment."

Harriet came in looking windswept. She pushed strands of hair behind an ear and sat down.

"Hello Jan, I'd love a cup of mint tea if there's any left." She took off her gloves and scarf putting them on the seat next to her bag and picked up the menu even though she knew it off by heart. "So how long are you here for?"

"Let's say in between foreign time. It's good to see you again Harriet, how come you're in homicide?" Harriet showed him her badge. "I didn't know. I'm impressed, well done. I hear things have been happening in the City of the Saints."

"Oh like what?"

"Like a string of people dying of natural causes that turns out to be the work of a serial killer."

Harriet leaned back and scowled. "Where did you hear that? Is that why you came to see me?"

Mitch smiled. "Well, well, so you're the investigating officer."

Harriet said nothing.

"Ok the Washington Post got a tip off and sent me to check it out. So that's why I'm in Salt Lake City but not why I'm here. We don't have to talk about that, how's your folks?"

"Ready to order?" asked Jan.

"Chicken Caesar salad with Guacamole please Jan. They're fine."

"Fries?"

Harriet shook her head. "Tempura mushrooms and onions?"

Jan sighed. "Rabbit food for sparrows again and for sir?" she said looking at her pad.

"Burger and blue cheese, thanks." Jan scurried off. "She doesn't like me, why?"

"She's my surrogate mother, thinks you're not good enough for me. Ok spill. What's your source."

Mitch picked up the salt condiment and placed it near Harriet. "I give you a little and you…," he placed the pepper next to his knife and fork, "…give me a little."

"How about this," she said moving the salt closer. "You give me it all and I won't arrest you for with-holding evidence. Be straight with me Mitch this is not a game. Someone's tried to kill me twice and they're not finished."

Jan arrived and put the plates on the table, "enjoy."

"When, what happened?"

Harriet toyed with the salad while Mitch stared at her. "Someone thought it would be a good idea shoving my car into a line of traffic."

"I can't help you with the source I honestly don't know. It may have come from a bereaved family member interviewed by a colleague of yours."

"Mitch what you're getting into is very risky. There has already been an investigative…never mind, go back to Washington tell them it's too dangerous."

"Does that sound like me?" Mitch took her hand.

"Who have you spoken to? If you do this you need a cover story. Start asking questions and flashing your government press ID in this town and you'll be another sudden death."

"What? I don't understand."

"It's a very complicated case and I cannot give out information on a live investigation. However if you create a plausible cover identity that will get you closer to what's going on, maybe you'll get some answers without raising suspicions. Keep in contact by dropping notes in my PO Box don't use emails or texts. When this is over you can break the story it'll take time believe me it's worth it. Oh and its best we're not seen together after this."

Harriet pushed open the door of empty briefing room three using her elbow with one hand carrying a laptop and the other a coffee. She sat down and opened it clicking on her email client. Up came a list in her inbox but she quickly found the one she was looking for and clicked on it.

'Sully,
Attached is Joe Simmons finished article written the day before he died that I retrieved from the tablet. It's self-explanatory but there are gaps in it, some guesswork and one or two assumptions. It's based around Bailey and Bailey's alleged activities in South America, US, Vietnam and Australia.
B.'

Harriet opened the attachment as the others came in and as they sat down she read it out loud.

'The Great Rare Earth Mineral Scramble.
The world has a very limited and dwindling reserve of extremely rare minerals. They are extensively used across all of modern scientific research and development including aerospace, arms manufacture and medical advances, Nano and quantum computer technology and much more. China is the world's largest producer at 90% but uses 60% domestically and is looking to restrict exports. However I have managed to ruffle the feathers of one American company based in Utah that is seeking to corner the market in rare earth minerals outside of China. Bailey and Bailey International Commodities Broker Incorporated have been busy buying various companies throughout the world such as Empresa de Minerais de Terras Raras in Brazil. It produces 95% of the world's Niobium which is used in superconductors and superconducting magnets and it also has substantial deposits of Tantalum. America has to import both these elements crucial to UD Defense Systems. Bailey and Bailey also have extensive interests in Australia, Vietnam, Malaysia and closer to home, California and in their home state Utah. The highly secretive nature of the industry may account for some of the reception I received at Bailey and Bailey head offices in Salt Lake City however I was surprised at being escorted from the premises by security guards wearing guns. But before then I did manage to ask the CEO Mr Clive Bailey about the long term security of supply for the American market and whether that was driving his acquisitions but he declined to comment citing market sensitive information. I also asked him how his company persuaded these mining companies to relinquish their ownership on such valuable resources given that they were unlikely to do so without good corporate necessity. The interview was abruptly terminated and an off the record statement was subsequently issued from their press office threatening legal action, requesting an embargo on the story until they had enough time to respond and requesting information on contacts. There is

also an MOU memorandum of understanding between Bailey and Bailey and Universal Defence and Development Contractors. Bailey and Bailey now appear to own the vast bulk of non-Chinese companies producing rare earth minerals in the world ensuring an uninterrupted supply for American industry.'

She looked at Jeff. "He didn't have a clue. Go up to a lion and poke him with a stick but don't be surprised if he eats you. He didn't know what kind of beast he was dealing with. Strange he was never warned about the danger."

"I don't agree Sully, he wasn't a stupid man. I think he was doing exactly as you say, poking the lion with a stick. That last sentence is almost coded. *'ensuring an uninterrupted supply for American industry'* That was completely out of context, what was he suggesting?" Jeff stood up and went to the window placing his hands on the glass. "What if there are those in the Department of Defense who are covertly supporting the consortium? It would make perfect sense. *'ensuring an uninterrupted supply for American industry'* What if these companies have been given a free reign as long as it's in the national interest. It could explain how so many gunmen could enter the country without being noticed."

"What about the FBI, the CIA and Homeland Security? We have no idea what they're doing, why?"

"Because they're not doing anything. This whole thing could go as high as the oval office."

There was a stunned silence. Harriet closed her laptop stood up and wiggled her phone and put it on the laptop the others followed suit. "I have to go to the bathroom I'll be back in a minute." She took them into her desk drawer and returned to the briefing room. "Just a precaution," she said entering. "Detective Barry what's your first name?"

"Desmond, Des."

"Des, Joan." She looked at Jeff and back at the others. "You have heard enough that could make you all targets. You have to be especially careful about what you say to colleagues and your line managers. I have the authority from the Sergeant for us to pursue this case without reporting to a senior officer every five minutes. I know this is unusual but the reason is that there is at least one person in this building who was either feeding information to Simmons or getting information. The explosion in the evidence bureau was no accident. Now we are going to try and piece together what we know about the sudden deaths and whether there were any links with the two companies under investigation or any mining companies."

Joan took out her notebook and rifled through the pages. "I kept a secondary list of sudden deaths that had no connection to the three companies and I think there was someone who died in a helicopter crash in Newfoundland." She found the page. "Yes here he is Dr Paul Croxon listed because he was born in Brigham. He was production manager of Astro Mining near Isabella Falls. Company share price soared after they discovered sizeable amounts of eudidymite, joaquinite, astrophyllite and karnasurtite. All rare earth deposits."

"What's the betting it's now owned by Bailey and Bailey," said Harriet.

One by one they all gave their reports and it became clear a pattern was emerging that was beyond coincidence.

"I think we have enough information to instigate an investigation into these deaths and I will be submitting a report to Grainger. Good work everyone you are now part of an unofficial unit to look into serial contract killers and their clients. We'll start with Bailey and Bailey. Jeff I'm going off to see one of these mining companies, you will be the team leader and co-ordinate a work load. I want to know the corporate structure of Bailey and Bailey. What it owns and how? I want as much background as you can get on Clive Bailey and his brother. Now we do have one major problem. If we flag up any signs of our investigation within the CIA, FBI or Homeland Securities, we'll be shut down at best or simply pushed under a bus. This is going to have to be old fashioned policing. Do not leave a digital trail. Do not use cell phones. Tablets and computers must be used offline. In the morning go to your bank and withdraw enough cash for the days' expenses if needs be use a cheque, it takes several days to clear. Do not use cash machines, debit cards or credit cards. Keep receipts, you will be reimbursed. If anybody has a smart watch leave it at home, GPS navigation in their car switch it off. I am already under scrutiny and that's one of the reasons why I'm going on a trip. I will be leaving a clear digital trail so they will be more interested in me than you. What puzzled Joe Simmons is why a small mining company in Brazil allowed themselves to be taken over? Ok I think we've covered everything now. Your phones and tablets are in my desk drawer I suggest you switch them off and take them home, thanks guys."

16

"Grainger I want to go to Brazil."

He looked at her without replying and leaned back in his chair. There was a weary tiredness that seemed to always overtake him when Harriet came into his office. Pushing and probing the system always testing until something twanged in his mind something that could be noticed upstairs. One of these days she would really land him in it if he wasn't careful but the face he looked at was oblivious to the horrible convoluted politics he had to endure and deal with on a daily basis. He sighed and raised his eyebrows questioningly.

"There's a lead I have to follow."

He scratched the back of his head and let out a funny short laugh. "Sully the last time I looked at a map, Brazil was in South America not in Utah has anything changed that has passed me by since my school days?"

"As I said to you Simmons tablet lodged with the evidence bureau was a plant Ben kept the real one in his safe and managed to get into the hard drive. There was a very interesting if limited article which had a reference to a mining company in Brazil. It currently holds 95% of the world's reserves of Niobium a very rare mineral. For some unaccountable reason they sold out to Bailey and Bailey. This whole investigation is not just about murder it's also about the acquisition of small mining rare earth producers throughout the world by hook or by crook. I think the government is aware of Bailey and Bailey's dodgy business practise and its use of contract killers and it's turning a blind eye because of the scarcity of rare minerals. It's all here in my report."

"Whoa, Sully are you hearing yourself."

"The evidence is stacking up and it's pointing to a state department conspiracy."

"You're in homicide."

"It's all linked. The murders are only the end product that we've stumbled on. This rare minerals business is really what is generating all these murders and they won't stop, you can see that Grainger can't you? We have to stop these killings."

"Are you crazy? I can't authorize your trip to Brazil. If you go, you pay for it yourself and as a private individual you'll have no special rights, you don't represent the department in any way shape of form. But there's another thing...," the phone rang. "Hello Chief."

"Grainger, where's Sullivan?"

"Well she's sitting at the other side of my desk."

"What is she doing?"

"Still working away with the sudden deaths cases."

"Any progress?"

I think it's still too early, do you want to speak to her? Ok I'll tell her." He put the phone down. "He says good luck."

"What's the other thing?"

"If what you're saying is even half right you'll be an easy target. I can't protect you. There'll be internal questions. The Chief keeps checking, says the Mayor is breathing down his neck."

"Grainger, I'm getting really stressed with this case, I need a couple of days in the sun. Maybe somewhere abroad like Brazil."

Grainger shook his head and smiled. "I want an updated report before you go, don't worry I'll hang on to it for a little while. Get outta here."

American Airlines flight from Miami arrived early at Belo Horizonte's Tancredo Neves International Airport. By global standards it wasn't a particularly big airport which made it easier to negotiate walkways and escalator towards passport control. Harriet didn't have long to wait in the queue to present her passport to the immigration officer. He looked at her and the photograph, scanned the passport into a computer, scanned it again under a UV light and studied his monitor.

"You are in the wrong queue this is for Brazilians."

Harriet looked around to see he was right. "I'm sorry," she said reaching out for her passport.

He waved her hand away. "Purpose of visit?" he asked without looking at her.

"Tourism."

"We don't get many tourists in Belo Horizonte." He reached for something under the counter. "Can you wait just there please?" he gestured towards a red lined square. "Next," he shouted. Two men in dark suits arrived at the passport control desk. The immigration officer handed over her passport. They looked over at her and approached.

"Miss Sullivan could you come with us please?"

One led while the other took her flight bag and followed behind making their way through several security doors. As they went deeper into the building the corridors and doors became scruffier and narrower, paint was peeling from the walls and bare white strip-lights cast cold shadows as they passed.

Harriet recognised an unmistakeable line of cells and beyond an interview room. The door was held open and as she entered she looked round the small room with the obligatory two way mirror on the wall a table and two chairs and then the door clanged shut. Harriet sat down. An hour passed then another. Harriet recognised the classic interviewing technique and sat passively with her eyes closed, her hands clasped together on her lap showing no emotion aware that every action was being viewed. But inside her mind was racing, the questions tumbling over each other vying for attention. She pushed them aside and attempted to reach a state of peace and meditative calm. 'Meditation was good for the soul,' she could hear her tutor saying. Wherever you are it is possible to reach the inner you. All it takes is concentration, focussed concentration. Visualise a wall, a brick wall, the colour, texture grain of the casting the cement holding one to the other and that's important because one, as in life does not make a whole. Keep that vision until the cement disappears, the colour drains, and the texture fuses together until you have nothing.

The door opened with a bang but still with her eyes closed there was no reaction. Four men came in. One stood at the door, two walked round her chair and stood behind her while the fourth man took off his jacket and draped it over the back of the empty chair wafting a distinctive deodorant towards her. She opened her eyes. He put a clipboard with a pad, a pen and her passport on the table and sat down. Picking up her passport he leafed through the pages. She waited with her hands still clasped on her lap for it to begin.

"My name is Captain Flavio Ribeiro," he said with a flourish. He was young good looking with a thin immaculately trimmed moustache, slicked black hair and brown eyes. He slowly turned page after page as if there was some clue some inkling of her real presence in his country written on one of them. "You are still airside, not yet in Brazil therefore you are not subject to any legal rights." He said each word, each syllable slowly. "You are in effect in limbo land. This passport is due for renewal. It expires in June." He looked at her. "You don't travel much do you? What are you doing in Brazil?" He turned a page of the Passport, "Harriet? You can call me Flavio."

"I've come to enjoy your wonderful country."

Flavio took a pack of cigarettes out took one placed it behind an ear and put the pack on the table clasping his hands together He gestured at the pack. She shook her head in reply.

"Why not the beaches of Rio de Janeiro or the architecture and nightlife of Brasilia or the rainforests of the Amazon?" he shrugged his shoulders. "Belo Horizonte?" He took the cigarette from behind his ear and lit it sending a plume of blue smoke upwards. "Have you ever smoked...filthy habit I intend to give up on the birth of my third child. So," he said picking a piece of tobacco from a tooth. "What are you really doing here?"

"There is a zoo that has some very rare animals that I would like to see and take photographs of."

"We have many zoos in the country."

"This is a private zoo."

"Do you have any children?" Harriet shook her head. "Married?"

"No."

"I am blessed with a wonderful wife and two little angels and I can't wait for the third. When I go home the little ones ask me... what did you do today daddy? You know what I do? I lie." he shook his head. "I lie, why? Because I want to protect them. From what? Life? Brazil? Reality? No. I want to protect their innocence. There is time enough in the future when they will know what I do. I'm surprised you have no children. In Brazil you would be a grandmother. Brazil is a very dangerous place but there are only two institutions that are most dangerous, our prisons and here.

I'll be honest with you, I'm not a bad person, but I have a job to do. In your case I am genuinely concerned about your safety and believe me I am not overstating that," he looked at his watch. "I have plenty of time Harriet, do you? When my shift ends …," he looked at his watch again, "…in an hour I go home have lunch with my lovely family, what will you be doing?"

"It is owned by Empresa de Minerais de Terras Raras and I'm particularly interested in Maned Wolves. They live in the grasslands and eat snakes."

Flavio started laughing that turned into a cough. He stubbed out the cigarette leaving a thin ribbon of blue rising from it. "That's good," he coughed again, "that's very good. What is your occupation?"

"I'm Detective Harriet Sullivan a homicide Detective from Salt Lake City Police Department."

Flavio nodded, "and you have a particular interest in what did you call them? Maned Wolves?"

"I watch wildlife programmes."

"You know Brazil has over fifteen thousand kilometres of borders with ten countries…" He unclipped a clear folder that was behind the notepad and took out some photographs placing them one by one in front of Harriet and in the process waved his hand to emphasize the words. "…and there are millions of ways drug smugglers can enter and ply their trade. There are routes into Venezuela which is the pipeline, the conduit to North America." He finished and looked at her. "Study these photographs carefully do you know any of these men?"

Harriet didn't alter her gaze from him. "No."

Flavio sighed and gathered the photographs together then stood up. "Is there anything I can get for you?" Harriet shook her head. Flavio looked at his watch again. "You know my replacement…

his English isn't very good and between you and me he has little patience. He's also very clumsy. People tend to get hurt... accidentally of course." He put on his jacket and picked up the cigarette pack and the clipboard then sat on the corner of the table looking down at her. "We have information that you are due to meet one of Colombia's most successful drug traffickers."

"And you got this information from the American Drug Enforcement Agency who got it from the FBI and we are no doubt waiting for the DEA to come and arrest me. It'll come as a great surprise to my bosses who will start asking some very serious questions to some very high up people which is of course absolutely no concern of yours. You're just doing your job."

Flavio sat down. "Ok," he said with both hands outstretched and then whispered. "Actually I didn't believe their story and I don't believe yours. So what is really going on?"

"You're an intelligent man Flavio. If I told you it is very much in the interest of Brazil that I am released so that I can go to the Empresa de Minerais de Terras Raras will you let me go?"

Flavio pursed his lips and studied her. "Can you be more specific?"

"There is a big gap between what I think may be true and what I know to be true."

"Try me."

"I suspect that an American company has somehow got control of this mining company in Brazil and they are illegally shipping rare earth minerals into America."

"You really want to go to this... Empresa?"

"Yes. Incidentally they do have a private zoo, not the best of cover stories admittedly but it could have worked. Hopefully we'll get the answers there. I know it's a slim chance but I don't have many options."

"Ok, let's go. Never mind the zoo you'll have me. What's the point of climbing through the window when you can open the front door?"

17

From the guard house barrier the coiffured landscape surrounding the mine was immaculate with hardly a blade of grass daring to grow longer than regulation height. Two tall blond women in uniform came out one at either side of the car and began a conversation in Portuguese with the driver. A badge was flashed, a call made from inside and they were allowed to proceed. They slowed down in silence to look at two mounted guards both blond women on superb reddish brown thoroughbred horses walk by.

Flavio waved at the women. "A boys' fantasies come true," he said.

They stopped outside a three storey building clad in tinted glass. It could have been a university campus or a bond villains' headquarters. They were met by another beautiful long haired woman in a pink suit who led them inside the air conditioned building and up a wide spiral staircase to an open office where a young well-dressed man rose from a large antique satinwood desk.

"Captain Ribeiro and Detective Sullivan," he offered his hand. "This is an unexpected pleasure, would you like some refreshment?"

"No I think were fine Señor Cabral it is good of you to see us at such short notice. My colleague cannot stay long in the country."

"Please have a seat." He beckoned towards leather chairs around a coffee table. "What can I do for you?"

Flavio looked at Harriet who took out her phone pressed record and put it on the table. "Señor Cabral, forgive me what's your position in the company and how long have you been here?"

"I am the Managing Director and I've been in the job since it was taken over six months ago."

"Who was the previous MD?"

"It was Miguel Barroso."

"I'd quite like to speak to him do you have a contact address?"

"That won't be possible I'm afraid he had a terrible death, he was bitten by an armadeiras."

Harriet looked at Flavio. "Eh, Armadeiras...Wandering Spider. It's the most venomous spider in the world."

"What about his family?"

"Yes my secretary will give you all the details."

"Señor Cabral I want to ask you some very important questions that may be market sensitive but I can assure you that none of your competitors will know anything about our conversation."

He laughed. "We don't have any competitors."

"You produce Niobium?"

"Yes and Tantalum."

"Where is your market for Niobium? Who do you sell it to?"

The smile faded replaced with an almost imperceptible nervous tic at the corner of his mouth.

"Well we have many customers for Niobium."

Harriet cleared her throat. "It's considered internationally as a strategic mineral and it's listed on the American Critical Materials Strategy document making it a very important mineral for America. Brazil has an 80% export tax on Niobium and a 30% tax on Tantalum. How much of your production officially and unofficially goes to America now that your company has been taken over?" she asked.

There was a very awkward silence. "I don't have the authority to give you that information." Despite the air conditioning he was visibly sweating now.

Harriet gaze never altered. "Señor Cabral It is highly likely that Miguel Barroso was murdered. I have been investigating a series of murders connected to your parent company. I believe that Empresa de Minerais de Terras Raras has been shipping large amounts of Niobium to America contrary to the laws and export rules of Brazil."

Flavio began talking in Portuguese in little more than a whisper when his cellphone rang. He answered it listened then rang off.

"Your friends from the DEA are waiting for you at the airport but this is very interesting, we shall make them wait." He turned and looked at Señor Cabral, "well?"

"They will kill me," he whispered

"They will not know, of course if you prefer Pedrinhas Prison." He looked at Harriet. "It's a jungle, be-headings, male rape, riots, turf wars, the wardens have no control."

"I didn't know they killed Miguel. 70% of Niobium production is exported without the correct documentation to America. It is listed as fertilizer and travels in sealed containers by ship. It's unloaded at the container terminal Port of Los Angeles in San Pedro after that I don't know."

"The US has the most efficient and rigorous import controls in the world how can anyone possibly smuggle in such huge amounts of Niobium?" asked Harriet.

"You don't know?" He asked. Harriet shook her head. "Bailey and Bailey have very influential friends in Washington. How else would it be possible?"

"Influential friends, who?"

Señor Cabral looked around nervously licking his dry lips.

"Which department?" she asked. Cabral looked away.

"Which department?" Flavio spoke softly in Portuguese.

"*Defense*." Harriet barely hear the word. "Do you have a name?"

He shook his head. "That's all I know."

She picked up her phone and pressed stop. "I think were done here," she said to Flavio.

"For now," he said standing up. "Até logo Señor."

It was getting hot outside as they walked to the car. Flavio's colleagues had the engine running and the air condition on. They got into the back seat and it pulled away. "Do you want to see Barroso's widow?"

"No it's a familiar story just a different method."

"Why is the DEA after you?"

"It's a long story. They just want me to disappear. There is a huge conspiracy within the US government and it's all connected to the continued supply of Niobium and other strategic rare minerals that are on the critical list. The company, Bailey and Bailey International Commodities Broker Incorporated is based in Salt Lake City and as you heard own this mine. They illegally import Niobium and launder it through their company network stockpiling and distributing it to defence manufacturers like Universal Defence and Development Contractors. Many people have died to ensure America maintains her supply. If you hand me over to them I'm dead too."

"Your flight bag is in the trunk." He handed her passport over. "We will be investigating the death of Miguel Barroso and when I submit my report, the government will be informed of the illegal export of rare minerals. Harriet you have done this country a great service, what would you like me to do for you?"

The traffic stopped at a busy junction where traders with stalls were selling all manner of goods. Shoppers were lined along the side-walk spilling out and narrowing the road. With a natural dislike of air conditioning Harriet wound the window down a little. Music and excited chatter filtered through along with the faint but unmistakeable sound of a helicopter. Flavio said something and the radio crackled into life. He opened the door and looked up.

"That's strange there's a Military Police helicopter immediately above us."

"It's an American armoured Bell Huey II we use them in Utah." She looked at Flavio. "Are we being targeted...?" There were two metallic pings and both men in the front slumped forward held by their seatbelts. Flavio pulled Harriet over kicked open his door and disappeared into the crowd followed by Harriet. She heard some rapid fire and a couple in front of her fell to the ground. People were screaming and running for shelter. Harriet could feel the downdraught of the helicopter as she ran through the crowd. She screamed as she was pulled into a narrow alleyway and just as she was about to lash out saw Flavio. He had his pistol out looking upwards.

"Phone." Harriet took it out and ejected the SD memory card and gave it to him. He dropped it on the ground along with his own and stamped on them. The sounds of police sirens got louder as the helicopter moved away. She followed him along the alleyway until they emerged into a busy street. Flavio hailed a cab said something to the driver and they sped off. The streets narrowed and the speed increased until they entered a Favela on the outskirts of Belo Horizonte. Fragile looking corrugated lean-to homes, naked toddlers with runny noses sitting on steps, chickens squawking and scurrying out of the way as they passed leaving feathery wisps behind, anxious looking teen girls eyeing the cab with suspicion as it went by, rubbish at the side of the track and sewage running down the middle, this was a world Harriet had never imagined let alone seen.

They passed a stream lined with small huts raised on stilts and then the cab stopped. The track was too narrow for it to go any further. Harriet and Flavio got out. "Obrigado." He said paying the driver. They walked on through the drying clothes hanging from make-shift polls suspended from huts. Cables spread from hut to hut carrying stolen electricity. This was Aglomerado Morro do Papagaio, perhaps not as big as the Favelas in some larger cities but just as pock marked with poverty. A no go area run by drug dealers and pimps, the only law enforcement was at the whim of local gang leaders. The incline steepened slowing them down for a few moments to catch their breath. A woman of indeterminate age wearing a very tight yellow pair of shorts and polka dot top was smiling leaning against an advertising hoarding breastfeeding a young toddler.

At the entrance of a small store a friend wearing a short blue skirt and red top kissed the baby in her arms, naked except for a diaper. Bare footed five year old s stared at them in silence unchecked by their parents. A goat wandered by unseen. Somewhere a dog yelped. They continued uphill until they reached a bigger than usual newly painted blue hut. Flavio opened the door and walked in while Harriet hesitated. He came back and beckoned. Harriet took her shoes off. The hard smooth undulating earthen floor bore witness to generations of bare feet. In the corner next to a small window a figure sat holding a smoking pipe in one hand and a chimarrão filled gourd spouting a silver stem in the other.

"This is Maria Clara my mothers' sister," he said sitting on a small stool next to her.

The aromatic Irlandez tobacco smoke cleared enough for Harriet to see a diminutive woman with small eyes observing her. She sucked on the stem of the gourd with a gurgling sound drinking the strong local tea and took another puff from the pipe exhaling the blue smokescreen. Flavio began talking while she listened in silence. Then she whispered something. Flavio hesitated looking slightly embarrassed at Harriet and said. "Na."

"What was she asking?" asked Harriet.

"My aunt wanted to know if you are married."

Harriet smiled. Maria Clara was also smiling showing broken mate stained teeth attached to red gums.

"Flavio is there internet can I send an email?"

He gestured towards the meagrely furnished room.

"Sorry," she said feeling a little stupid.

"You can stay the night here and I will be back in the morning. If there is a problem and I do not return before breakfast you must leave here and go to a friend of mine. He is an Egbomi, an elder of the Candomblé faith, he will help you. His name is Dr Marcos Vinicius Teixeira. I have explained to Maria Clara, she will ensure you get to him. He is a good man he will help you."

"What about you?"

"Someone thinks I'm dispensable. Now I will try to find out who and get to him first before he gets to me."

"If I had known coming to Brazil would have resulted in more killings I wouldn't have come."

Flavio looked at Harriet in surprise and laughed. He got up from the stool and sat next to her. "Brazil has the highest murder rate in the world. Do you know how many people were slaughtered in my country last year, Mm?"

"No."

"Almost 65,000 in one year. That's nearly five times more than the murders in the whole of the United States. Tomorrow, if I cannot be with you when you are travelling you may see things you do not understand and you will certainly see things you do not like. Remember, you are a passive observer nothing else."

18

The darkness came quickly and so did sleep despite barking dogs and distant Maracatu music. In the morning Café da Manhã was a simple affair with Mandioca crepe tapioca filled with cheese and exotic Amazonian fruits. Toasted Pão francês spread with butter was accompanied with strong black coffee and while Harriet ate breakfast Maria Clara talked in Portuguese. She may have been telling Harriet what a splendid fellow Flavio was, perhaps good marrying material, or she could have been passing comment on the weather or her health, Harriet could only guess. The nice thing was that she didn't ask any questions and didn't expect any replies. There was a tap at the door and the small brown face of a ten year old boy peered in. When he saw Harriet he grinned from ear to ear put the stick he was carrying under one arm and saluted.

"*Olá Como está? Meu nome é Raul*, Raul, *Significado* wise wolf," he puffed up his chest. "*E estou dez anos* um, ten years old. I am *acqui*, here *Ter você*, take you to the Egbomi, Casa Antiga Pedra Cinzenta." He looked a little weary with the effort but managed another wide grin.

Harriet finished her breakfast, "*obrigado.*"

"*Obrigada,*" he corrected.

Maria Clara raised herself from the chair and Harriet got up and gave her a hug. "*Muito obrigada Maria Clara.*"

"*De nada. Boa sorte, Boa viagem, Cuidado.*" She held her hand.

"Harriet, Flavio very good man."

"Yes he is."

Maria Clara let go. "*Adeus.*"

Raul took her hand and they left. It had rained during the night. The air was crisp and clean, the colours of the dwellings deceptively bright and optimistic. A gaggle of geese passed in front of them screeching and hissing herded by a small girl with a thin stick picking her nose and staring. Naked children screamed as they jumped up and down in a rain filled catchment tub. Women were hanging out there washing while menfolk were conspicuously absent. Harriet wondered what the life expectancy was in the Favela there were not many older people. A rumble of thunder unusual so early in the morning echoed down the hillside. Somehow it didn't seem at all strange to Harriet that she was being led by a ten year old boy to an unknown destination. It was getting hotter. They turned a corner and not more than ten yards away two policemen, one sitting astride a motorcycle the other beating a teenager in handcuffs.

He stopped and looked at Harriet. Raul launched himself at her with his arms around her neck and started crying. "*Mãe eu não quero ir para a escola.*" She held him close squeezing passed the policemen while black vultures shoulder wrestled for scraps on a nearby midden and turkey vultures patrolled high above with their characteristically unsteady flight scenting the freshly dead. Rounding a corner Harriet put a grinning Raul down. The lane narrowed then widened into a small square where two youths sharing a hammock were injecting. They swung gently lost in synthetic pleasure. A small dog came out from a shed and started barking. Raul waved his stick and it sat down. They made their way towards a grey brick two storey house on the far side of a square. They stopped at a sturdy green double door each with four moulded wooden panels separated by black painted wrought iron straps and iron ring handles. Raul banged on the door and just when Harriet had given up one half opened.

"Ah Harriet do come in." Dr Marcos Vinicius Teixeira smiled and stood aside. He wore a crisp white shirt and blue jeans. His shaven face looked fresh and young yet he had grey hair and rimless glasses.

"Olá Raul como está?"

"Há quanto tempo!"

"He is a fine boy is he not?" he said closing the door. "Come through, would you like some coffee?"

"Thank you, it's very kind of you to see me."

"I haven't done anything yet, please sit."

Harriet sat at the kitchen table with her back to the window and looked around the room. A woman took two cups from a wall shelf and poured out coffee from a shiny aluminium percolator that had been heating on a propane gas stove. It was cool inside helped by a random mosaic marble stone floor and open glassless wooden window shutters at both ends of the kitchen. A string of onions hung next to the shelves and beside that a grimy large pale green 1950's refrigerator hummed in the corner. Dr Teixeira sat opposite her and opened a leather folder, Raul sat at the end. The woman put the cups on the table.

"Have you heard from Flavio?" she asked.

The woman opened the fridge and took out a small bottle of cola for Raul who beamed with anticipation.

"No. But he is a very resourceful man, he must have been delayed."

"Did he tell you anything about my situation?"

"He didn't need to, only that you need help. That was enough for me. I am in debt to Flavio and I always will be."

Harriet drank the strong black coffee and thought for a minute. She didn't want to burden him with everything that had happened. "While I remain in Brazil my life and anyone that happens to be connected to me is in danger. I have to leave the country without my passport being electronically checked."

"That is easy, do you have any money?"

"Only a few dollars. I lost my flight case."

"Ok." He started scribbling. "I will give you five hundred and fifty US this is my email address you can use PayPal to transfer the money when you get home."

He looked at her and tore off the details passing them over. Raul started whistling. He looked bored not being able to follow the conversation. "*Raul.*" He stopped. "Ok on the last Brazilian mile of the Amazon River you will travel by boat, cross the border into Colombia and it will keep going until you get to Letitia. Then you can get a cab to take you to the Alfredo Vásquez Cobo International Airport where you board a flight to Bogota. From there you will get a connecting flight onwards. A word of caution. This route is used by gun smugglers, drug runners, people traffickers and murderers, it can be extremely dangerous. You have to be like all the other normal travellers, oblivious. Oh by the way…," he spoke to the woman in Portuguese. She opened a drawer and took out a newspaper handing it to him. Harriet's face was on the front page, "…you'll have to go in disguise you're all over the news. It says here you are an American drug trafficker caught in a gangland dispute while meeting the notorious drug dealer Leonardo Alejandro. They are speculating that you are dead. If it were true that would mean Flavio would be involved and I know that to be wrong. You do not have to explain anything. You will be alright in Colombia they don't read Brazilian newspapers."

"How long will the journey take?"

"Depending on connections you should be in the US in a day or so. You will travel as a foreign goodwill emissary from the Candomblé faith. These papers will not be questioned if you are stopped." He handed them to her along with the money. "I must make some phone calls and book your boat trip and flights."

The iron oxide red dust from the dirt road wheezed through a hole in the floor and every other chink of the battered Suzuki covering everything inside. Keeping the windows closed was pointless except when meeting an oncoming vehicle. It was hot allowing the dust to adhere to sweaty skin. The soft suspension was sleep inducing until the tyres found the odd hole. Corrugations forming through many passing cars and trucks, birled beneath them. Hugo the driver who spoke no English, alternately chewed coca leaf and spat out of the open window. There were many stops for fuel and food, a burst tyre, a fallen tree requiring a detour, water in the leaking radiator and stops to allow headaches from petrol fumes to clear. In the early evening, red and exhausted the pair finally arrived at a simple wooden pier where the triple deck riverboat *Rabbitinho de Rio* was berthed. Harriet paid, thanked and said goodbye to Hugo. She was shown a clean cabin with a mosquito net over the large bed and immediately took advantage of the tepid shower. Clean, she crawled under the net and fell asleep.

"Mitch?"

"Harriot, I didn't recognise your number."

"It's not my phone I bought this at the airport I'm glad you got my text thanks for calling me back, are you in a payphone like I said?"

"Yes."

"Good…"

"Where are you?"

"Never mind where I am just listen."

"They're reporting all sorts of…"

"…I know I know, don't believe anything you read in the newspapers."

"What happened are you Ok?"

"Yes I'm Ok it's a long story. Find Jeff."

"Who?"

"Jeff Blackwell and Sergeant Stokes and rustle up a film crew. Meet me at the airport, the flight is arriving from Mexico at 7pm tonight. I could have a problem getting through immigration and I need all the help I can get. You know what to do if they try and spirit me away, kick up a big fuss. Interview the head of immigration, the Mayor, the Chief, the DA, doorstep them if they won't agree to an interview. This is a massive story Mitch but I only have bits of the puzzle. I know what's going on but I need more evidence. I'm very grateful Mitch, thanks." She took the battery out of the phone, dropped it in the trash and bought another. Then she bought a pack of envelopes kept two and threw away the rest. She put the SD card into one and sealed it writing:

'Dad,
Please keep this safe until you hear from me. I'll explain later.
Love H
X'

She put it into the second envelope and wrote the address, found an airline shop selling stamps and posted the letter.

"I had a call from Harriet. She's flying into SLC from Mexico arriving approximately 7.0pm." Mitch took out a handkerchief and blew his nose.

Grainger looked at Jeff and stood up from behind his desk glowering. "There are reports of her being mixed up with the drug trade in Brazil. She was in the middle of a shoot-out leaving two Brazilian policemen dead along with a number of innocents, passers-by. Now she's posted missing presumed dead. Do you know what's going on?"

Mitch shrugged. "No more than you." He put the handkerchief back in his pocket. "She thinks she'll be stopped at immigration and wants you two to meet the flight."

"Mitch are you two working together?"

"Harriet and I? Absolutely not. You don't know her very well do you Grainger? She's in serious trouble otherwise she wouldn't have called me."

"We need some heavyweights in case the FBI are involved." He picked up the phone. "Chief I need to see you it's important."

"What about?"

"Detective Sullivan." He put the phone down. "Let's go."

Chief McLeod and District Attorney Wayne Spears were waiting as Mitch, Jeff and Grainger arrived.

"Who are you?" The Chief was rapping the table impatiently staring at Mitch.

"Mitchell, I'm Harriet's boyfriend…ex-boyfriend."

"Wait a minute, I know you, you're a journalist what are you doing in my office?"

"Cut him some slack Chief he got a call from Sully today," said Grainger.

"Ok. Sit down guys. Jeff get yourself a chair. Grainger what the hell was Detective Sullivan doing in Brazil?"

"She was unofficially following up a lead about sudden deaths."

"The idea that one of our homicide detectives is a drug dealer is frankly ludicrous," said the Chief.

"She is due in on the Mexico flight this evening and expects to be held by immigration," said Mitch.

"Is that all she said?"

"She said she knew what was going on but needed more evidence."

"Ok Mr Mitchell I thank you for that information and you can rest assured we will be doing the right thing by Sullivan and no, you can't quote me." The Chief got out of the chair and opened the door. "Jeff can you show Mr Mitchell out?" The door closed. "This whole thing stinks of the FBI. Ok Grainger what the hell is going on?"

"Someone high up in government is using the FBI to covertly support an international commodities broker who is using illegal means to take over rare earth mining companies and illegally import these minerals into the US on the grounds of strategic national defense. The company concerned is Bailey and Bailey International Commodities Brokers Incorporated. This company is now the sole supplier of rare earth minerals to the Universal Defence and Development Contractors Corporation. Sullivan was investigating seemingly sudden deaths and found at least fifteen had some connection with either company. Some were employees some were relatives of employees or contractors. Simmons draft piece pointed Sully to a Brazilian company that was taken over. It produces 95% of a very rare earth mineral. That's why she went there. What happened in Brazil I don't know but she would have been tracked."

Chief McLeod looked at his watch. "I hope you're right Grainger this is going to be one helluva ding-dong." He picked up the phone. "Hello who do we have at the airport?...Ok I want them in immigration. Let's go."

The DA leaned forward. "We'll have to let the Mayor know and the Governor."

Harriet finished her gin and tonic and looked out of the window as sheets of hail stones rushed by. The seatbelt signs went on. "Ladies and gentlemen this is the Captain we are waiting for clearance from the tower to land at Salt Lake City International Airport. There may be a certain amount of turbulence due to a localized storm."

Lightening flashed close by illuminating the interior of the cabin as the jet lost altitude and then stabilized. The woman next to her closed her eyes and gripped the arm rests.

"This is the Captain, there is not much to see outside but take it from me, below us is SLC. We should be landing in five to ten minutes."

An inexplicable feeling of euphoria swept over Harriet catching her by surprise. Maybe it was the alcohol or possibly relief that she had survived three attempts on her life and now she was almost home. Even the storm outside held no fears for her. The woman opened her eyes at the touch of Harriet's hand and was reassured by her smile. Outside there was still no sign of the city and yet Harriet could sense they were close to the runway. The wheels thumped down and the jet bounced then touching down again as the engine went into reverse thrust slowing them down. Through the hail storm flashing lights from several emergency vehicles approached the aircraft.

"Ladies and gentlemen welcome to Salt Lake City, can Miss Sullivan please make herself known to the cabin staff, thank you."

Harriet raised her hand and whispered to the woman next to her. "This is my welcoming committee."

A door opened chilling the cabin as Harriet made her way to the exit and down the steps, a black Range Rover flanked by two unmarked cars with blue flashing lights was waiting. A man opened the rear door allowing her in and followed her as she sat next to someone already there. They drove off around the perimeter fence and entered a hanger where a small jet was parked. Harriet was ushered out of the car up the steps and into the plane's cabin occupied by George Briscoe, two other men and two women. Her flight bag and jacket were taken from her then she was frisked. The contents of the bag were examined in detail. She was given a jump suit and told to strip.

"Can I have a little privacy?" she asked.

The men ignored her and examined her clothes for anything that might be hidden. One of the women officers began a strip search. They found a piece of paper.

"Who owns this email address, eixeiracandomble@hotmail.com and why do you have it."

She put on the jump suit. "You know that what you are all doing is entirely illegal?"

They handcuffed her and fastened her into a seat as the engines started. The executive jet taxied out of the hanger along a taxiway towards the runway and stopped waiting for permission to take off. The cockpit door opened and the co-pilot emerged.

"Sir we have been refused permission to take off. We have been ordered to return to the hanger."

"Take off!" said one of the men.

The co-pilot shook his head and went back to the cockpit. The jet turned and trundled back to the hanger. The man hammered on the locked door and kicked it as the plane stopped in the hanger with engines falling silent. He spoke on his phone and opened the door allowing the steps to fold out. Three cars appeared and Harriet was unbuckled and bundled once again into the back of the Range Rover. Her bag was thrown into the trunk. They drove in close convoy heading for a manned perimeter exit with a barrier. The barrier stayed down and two security guards approached the vehicles.

Harriet heard the driver of the lead vehicle shout. "FBI, lift the barrier."

"Sorry sir the airport is in lock-down no one in no one out. Can I see you're ID?"

Harriet's driver swore and took out his mobile. "We're having a problem leaving, fix it." Harriet sat in silence. There was no point asking questions they might not even know who she was. "You're obstructing FBI officers get that barrier up."

"I have my orders sir."

Six airport security cars pulled either side of the convoy blocking them in. Chief McLeod and Grainger got out and opened the rear doors of the Range Rover. "Chief McLeod SLCPD, out of the car." The men got out allowing Harriet to leave. "Keys!" Grainger took them and freed Harriet leading her to one of the security cars.

"You're making a big mistake Chief."

"Don't you guys know you have to go through the proper channels?"

He waved at the guard who raised the barrier. They got back into the car and with tyres screeching passed through the barrier into the night. The Chief got into the car and closed the door.

"Sully did you know you were going to attract all this attention in Brazil" Grainger was relieved and angry at the same time.

"That was one of the reasons I went. I left a trail. Passport checks, using my credit card and live GPS on my phone it was easy for them to track me but I didn't expect what happened."

"Save it for the debriefing. There are a lot of important people waiting to hear it. What is that you're wearing?"

Harriet closed her eyes and whispered, *"Thanks Mitch, I owe you."*

19

The Governor's office was surprisingly small. You could guess everything you needed to know about Samuel Hooker by analysing the contents of the shelves behind his leather topped desk. Calf bound copies of The Origins of Indigenous American Cultures, The Mayan Civilization, novels by Graham Greene, Hemingway and so on adorned the upper shelves. A display of photographs with the President, photographs of a wife with children, awards, a baseball glove, an ivory chess set, a Bible. It was the personal detritus of an important elected official's record of twelve years in public office, sterile to the outsider like most personal collections but priceless to the owner.

"Are you going to this debriefing Sam?"

"No and neither is my Lieutenant or the Mayor or you two. You know that no elected official can be seen to be interfering with the due process of the law," he said betraying his Texan origins. "If what I've heard so far is true and I only have an unsubstantiated report, Capitol Hill is in for one almighty shock."

Hooker looked at the two Utah Senators. Abigail (Abby) Robredo a professional politician groomed while studying law that had never worked outside politics. Matt McGuire had done it the hard way building up a construction business from nothing and selling it on for a healthy number of millions.

"Remind me, which committees are you on...Abby?"

"The House Committee on Natural Resources and also Transportation and Infrastructure."

"Matt?"

"Science space and Technology."

"Ok guys let's be clear whatever hits the fan either from Sullivan or from on high we need to cover each other's backs and maintain a neutral posture at least until we find out what the accusations are and more importantly what the evidence is. I know these guys at Universal Defence and Bailey and Bailey, hell they're members of the same club as me, and I have little desire to be rocking any boats."

Abby Robredo looked at Matt and cleared his throat. "I know these companies they have high powered lobbyists in Washington and many friends in very high places. This could get extremely messy."

"If a line has been crossed by the security agencies for whatever reason then it's up to the Whitehouse to sort it out. Now the FBI have already tried to arrest Detective Sullivan and I'm sure they are not going to go away. We need to steer clear of this. Once they have Sullivan's report there will no doubt be a damage limitation exercise plus a smear campaign. That young lady has no idea what is going to hit her. Keep a low profile don't use digital communication for anything connected to this and let's just wait and see what happens."

Harriet recognized most of the people in the briefing room. It was strangely quiet as Chief McLeod closed the door sat down and nodded to her. Harriet stood up.

"My investigation started with a sudden and unexplained death of a freelance investigative journalist called Joseph Simmons. Shortly after his death his wife Melissa Simmons was found dead in an apparent suicide. However the circumstances surrounding her death were highly questionable. She was left handed, the pistol was found in her right hand and there was no suicide note. Simmons tablet was retrieved from the river and IT managed to access the hard drive. An early draft of his report gave us a lead to a Brazilian company the Empresa de Minerais de Terras Raras in Belo Horizonte. This company has reserves of over 95% of the world's known deposits of Niobium. The then MD Miguel Barroso was bitten by a highly poisonous spider and died shortly before the company was taken over by Bailey and Bailey International Commodities Broker Incorporated. There are strict Brazilian export controls of this rare earth mineral. I have recorded evidence from the present MD of the company stating that 70% of Niobium and Tantalum exports are shipped without documentation to America. It is listed as fertilizer and travels in sealed containers by ship then unloaded at a container terminal in San Pedro. There are circumstantial links between an influx of contract killers from Eastern Europe who I believe were employed by both Universal Defence and Development Contractors Incorporated and Bailey and Bailey International Commodities Broker Incorporated. There are a number of unexplained sudden deaths and unlikely suicides linked to these companies. The dead either worked for them or had relatives working for them. These companies have an explicit interest in stockpiling dwindling world reserves of rare earth minerals. After I left this mining company in Brazil our car was attacked by a Military Police armoured Bell Huey II. Two police officers sitting in the front of our vehicle were killed. I managed to escape with the help of Captain Ribeiro." Harriet took a sip of water. "Someone wants me dead, they have tried three times. So, what is going on what is the bigger picture? Is it simply that we have, two rogue corporations? What about the DEA, FBI. Someone fed the newspapers in Brazil cock and bull stories about me being a drug dealer where did that come from? I don't believe that government agencies have become so unaccountable that they can act with impunity. These killings are not going to stop until we find out who is in overall control and I am in no doubt that someone high up in Government knows and condones…," the door opened and in came five men led by George Briscoe waving a piece of paper. Two walked over to Harriet, two quietly observed the people in the room, one stood by the door while Briscoe handed the paper to the Chief. The seated men stood up.

"…Now let's not get too excited guys this is a warrant for the arrest of Ms Sullivan signed by the Attorney General and all done through the proper channels."

The Chief read the warrant and looked at Harriet as she was handcuffed. "Are those necessary?"

Jeff was standing in the way near the door. "Grainger, Chief are you just going to let this happen?"

The Chief spread his arms in a gesture of impotence as they pushed passed and left.

The *Black Site* looked from the outside like a typical nondescript warehouse on the edge of a rundown rust belt collection of empty industrial factories in Detroit. This was the FBI's equivalent of the CIA's anonymous holding centres outside the US. Here people just disappeared from the judicial radar with no legal access. No-one was officially arrested or charged because this place was solely for interrogation. Specially trained interrogators using the latest techniques were highly skilled and successful at producing results. A large metal double door slid apart just wide enough to allow the vehicle through. Harriet was taken out and led to a small windowless cell where her handcuffs were removed. She hardly had time to look around the cell when the door opened. She was led through to an interview room where a familiar face was waiting.

"Harriet, you don't mind if I call you Harriet?" She sat down and looked across the table at Special Agent George Briscoe.

"Why am I here?"

"Let's get to know each other. You are my guest for the foreseeable future and I want to know what you know and then when I'm satisfied we're done and well, you can go home."

Harriet remembered hearing rumours about places like this. "And how many people from here make it home."

"Ah, not many it's true." He opened a thick file on the table and began reading. "It says here you're interested in art, so am I."

"Which interrogation technique is this...it's not John Reid?"

"I don't subscribe to these crude interrogation techniques. You know John Reid, the CIA's thirteen enhanced interrogation techniques used on detainees, that's a Guantanamo thing. No I'm just getting to know you."

She had put up a marker as if to say, you're not dealing with a pushover.

"I personally haven't got time for contemporary art," he said, "it's all over the place heading in all different directions influenced by just about anyone who ever picked up a brush. Daubs that's all they are...Emperor's clothes. No I prefer dead artists you know where you are with them...the market's tried and tested, it's almost like owning a promissory note to the value of whatever, would you like a coffee?"

"I have not broken the law."

Briscoe stifled a laugh. "Broken the law? I don't think you quite understand I have irrefutable evidence and witnesses who will testify about your drug dealing in Brazil," he leaned across the table and whispered, "I don't give a flying fig if you're innocent or not, it's irrelevant and I'm not in the slightest bit interested in that, where is the recording?"

"What recording?"

"You know you are facing a thirty year jail sentence."

"Charge me then."

"Are you being deliberately obtuse?" he leaned back in his chair. "All in good time Harriet you and I have embarked on a journey, isn't that exciting and only one of us knows where and when the journey will end. There are a number of scenarios that could be played out, but I'm getting ahead of myself." He tapped the folder. "It's all in here, your whole life story. I know more about you than I do about my own wife." He opened the folder. "You were very good at sports, tennis and swimming. You have a high IQ scoring 162, I could only manage 158." He shrugged. "How did you like Brazil?"

"So there's a carrot and there's a stick." she said, "They happened to be the same of course, pressing charges, not pressing charges and in return for what? You can't release me you know that. So another sudden death, suicide, mysterious illness, heart attack whatever. A poisonous spider, a helicopter crash, a fall from a high building its really very inventive don't you think. Are they your inventions? Is that what the FBI have become, a rogue agency killing innocent people for the good of the state? This is madness you know that. Too many people know now, the genie is out of the bottle. Save yourself and co-operate with SLCPD."

Briscoe's eyes widened. He started applauding with sincerity, beaming and nodding his approval. "Bravo, bravo, very, very good. We are going to have so much fun. It is rare that I meet an intellect like yours believe me. I frequently have to interview appallingly stupid people and I'm not very good at that. I feel sorry for them you see and it clouds my judgement. Alas I have my job to do. This business, it's like chess. When one strategy fails always have another up your sleeve. There is someone I would very much like you to meet." Keeping his eyes fixed on

Harriet he stood up and banged twice on the door then sat down again.

A few seconds later the door opened. Framed in the doorway, holding the hand of a female officer was a small girl with braided blond hair and blue eyes holding a knitted woollen doll. Harriet stood up a little shaken.

"Katya?" Instinctively the girl ran forward and threw her arms around Harriet sobbing. "If this girl has been harmed I swear..."

"...She's fine, a little tired with the journey and the uncertainty and of course missing her father and grandmother."

Harriet sat down with the girl on her knee and held her tight. "This is not chess, its barbaric involving a child. Katya, are you Ok?"

"Dzie moj baćka?"

"She's asking where her father is," said the female officer.

Harriet looked at Briscoe and then back at Katya. "Tell her, there will be time to explain but not just now."

"Are you a conspiracy theorist Harriet?"

Katya was sucking her thumb. Harriet thought for a moment. "Well George I don't believe that Elvis faked his own death and lives in Las Vegas impersonating himself, LBJ had Kennedy killed and the moon walk was filmed at Paramount studios if that's what you mean."

"Where are your investigations leading you to?" he asked.

"Do you have any idea what's going on?"

"Tell me."

"It doesn't bother you that innocent people are getting killed for the sake of the greater good? Tell you what, first I need to know what you know because I need to know where you stand." Katya had fallen asleep in Harriet's arms.

Briscoe pointed a finger at her and towards himself and back. "That's not the way this works. I ask the questions you answer."

"Ok."

"Ok let's start at the beginning why were you in Brazil?"

"I went to a zoo."

"I know where you went, I want to know why." He signalled to the female officer who came forward and took the sleeping child from Harriet.

"Ok I did it."

"Did what?"

"Plan to smuggle drugs from Brazil into the US. I had a meeting all lined up with Leonardo Alejandro for a big shipment. Ask the DEA and your bosses at the FBI, they concocted, I mean new all about that, that's why they tipped off the military police when I wasn't at the airport detention cell. An armoured helicopter was waiting for us and then the shooting began, five people killed I believe. I was tracked every step of the way, very careless of me but then I haven't had the same training or experience that you guys have. Charge me."

Briscoe slapped the flat of his hand on the table making Harriet jump and stood up. He was shaking. "You think this is just another game?" He leaned forward stretching the palms of his hands on the table. Recovering his composure he smiled and nodded. "You're right of course it is a game only this is no ordinary game because it has no rules and you're wrong about one thing you will leave here alive at least what I would call technically alive. I was researching for some inventive medical advice. What do you think would be the most appallingly slow and irreversible way to die? Go on have a guess." Harriet stared at him. "Total locked-in syndrome." He said slowly salivating over every syllable. "It's a paralysis that affects all the muscles including the eyes. You would have to rely on a ventilator to breath, intravenous feeding to stay alive. You will still have sensation being able to feel pain or pleasure for that matter. You will not even be able to blink but, on a more optimistic level your brain will function normally. You will be aware of everything. Total locked-in syndrome can be induced very easily in a number of ways. For example were you unlucky enough to be bitten by a snake in Brazil by any chance?" he shrugged his shoulders, "venomous neurotoxins are classic causes and there's no known cure, then there's curare poison from Brazilian Lianas." He shook his head. "Of course if a Doctor knew it was curare it could be reversed and who would tell him, you?" Harriet remembered the terrifying dream she had in the bath about Speedy Gonzales and shuddered.

"I think you've answered my question," she said, "let the girl go, she should be looked after by a foster family."

"We're all pawns in the game Harriet, pawns in the game. Now where were we? Ah yes, you know perfectly well I have no intention of charging you with anything so we've lost the carrot and the stick, shame. How can I persuade you that it would make everybody's life so much easier if you co-operated. I'd like to know where the recording is." Harriet stayed silent. "You were searched thoroughly what did you do with the recording you made of Señor Cabral? and exactly what evidence do you have, links, names, addresses telephone numbers..."

"...You're not interested in the sudden deaths or the contract killers from Belarus you want to know if I have names in the government."

"At last a glimmer of light, precisely so."

"I have none." Briscoe walked round the table looking down with his hands behind his back until he had returned to his seat.

"That was too easy an answer and immediately poses questions. Are you telling me the truth and how can I be sure? I personally don't like lie detector tests. While the exercise is entertaining it doesn't always work on higher IQs and it's time consuming. What about government departments?" Harriet shook her head. "Following up leads?" Harriet shook her head again. "You understand that this interview, you and me here and now, is only a preliminary. How old do you think I am?"

"Fifty-two?"

"Forty-four what does that tell you? Harriet there have been times in the past when I met a crossroad in my life where the gravity of a decision I had to take that would change my life wasn't fully understood because of my youth and inexperience. Make the right decision before it's too late."

"What kind of answer were you expecting? Who's pulling the strings George, how high up does it go?"

Briscoe pulled a pack of cigarettes from his pocket and put them on the table. "Smoke?" Harriet shook her head. "Neither do I, it's an interview prop." He opened her file again. "How's your boyfriend Mitchell?"

Harriet's eyes widened. "Ex, why?"

"Ah yes that's right, he's been digging quite a lot. Mostly a big hole for himself. He doesn't understand police methods. We are in the process of encouraging him to go back to entertainment journalism. And then there's your younger brother Jamie but you don't want to know what he gets up to. Why didn't you just walk away when you inherited all these millions? I don't understand it. We went to a great deal of trouble to make you rich. After everything that has happened on this journey I regretted his death the most. Never met him of course but I knew him better than he knew himself. Your progress in the SLCPD had been followed with great interest. Again it's a pity that you hadn't accepted our offer of a secondment, it might have saved your uncle's life. Remember Flavio? He told us about the recorded interview with Cabral. He's done well for himself promoted and sent from the suburbs of Belo Horizonte to the big time in Brasilia."

"I can't believe Flavio would do that," she said.

"Carrot and stick Harriet everyone has a choice and then there's the mysterious Teixeira. He's not on our radar and I don't suppose you are going to tell me who is."

Harriet looked round the room. "Could I have a drink of water?"

Briscoe ignored her request. "Joe Simmons. There wasn't time to give him a warning he got off the mark too quickly, shame. He didn't know the big picture but he was close. His wife's demise was a communication error, collateral damage I'm afraid. When you are dealing with different cultures, different languages who knows what will happen."

"How did Joe die?"

Briscoe waggled his finger and put it to his earpiece then looked at his watch. "Interview terminated at 12.22." He closed the folder stood up hammered on the door and turned to look at Harriet as it opened then left without a word.

20

FAO Karina Holsen, Washington Post

Missing Salt Lake City cop riddle
Exclusive by special correspondent Eliot Mitchell
Family and colleagues in Salt Lake City Police Department are becoming increasingly concerned at the whereabouts of Detective Harriet Sullivan after she was arrested by the FBI on alleged drug smuggling charges. The lack of information on the arrest has meant that family lawyer Frank Calderwood has been unable to determine where she is being held thwarting her rights for legal representation. "I think in this day and age in the United States of America it is truly shocking that the authorities can simply make someone disappear. Family members are extremely worried about how she is being treated and they do not believe that this is acceptable police procedure. I have made numerous attempts to locate Ms Sullivan through the FBI with no success therefore I have lodged papers with the Salt Lake City Justice Court requesting that the FBI release my client or charge her." Family members are appealing to the Governor of Utah to help track down Ms Sullivan. Her lawyers have stated that there has been no response to this request so far. A source from SLCPD has given a statement with the proviso not to be identified saying that there were real concerns for the safety of Ms Sullivan who has already survived three attempts on her life this month. When a request was made for a statement the District Attorney's office made no comment. A news blackout has been imposed by the police department about the circumstances of her arrest which happened while she was on a live homicide investigation into the

sudden deaths of a number of individuals in Utah.
Ends.

News Editor Steven Jessel of the Washington Post slung his jacket over the back of the chair sat down and typed in his username and password. "What on earth is the FBI up to? It looks like Sullivan has been rattling a few cages. It's a good piece from Mitch but it's not enough." He looked over his glasses at Chief reporter Karina Holsen. "Get hold of him. He needs to flesh it out he's asking questions with very little answers like for example what the hell is this all about?"

"I tried earlier when it first came through. He has been rushed to the University Of Utah Hospital seriously injured they've described his condition as critical. A neighbour found him lying at the bottom of his apartment stairs unconscious late last night. X-rays are showing a fractured skull and a broken leg. He still hasn't regained consciousness they say it's a fifty-fifty."

"What? Something smells. Wasn't this missing cop Sullivan, Mitch's girlfriend?"

"Yea they were going to get engaged then he went off for six months to Europe for the New York Times, really pissed her off."

"Where is her family?"

"Mom and Dad live in Florida, I've got the address here."

"Get a local stringer round there and when you've done that get your things together you're going to Utah. I've got a feeling about this story. I'll cover it from this end, the FBI have some explaining to do." Jessel picked up the phone and dialled the FBI National Press Office. "Is that Gerry? Hi Steven Jessel, there's a story we're running in tomorrow's paper and I've been looking through your press releases but there's no mention of it."

"Which story?"

"It's about the arrest of a homicide Detective, her name is Harriet

Sullivan from Salt Lake City PD, do you know anything about it?

"No and that's why it's not on our list. I'll dig into it and call you back."

"Sure but there's not much time, thank anyway." He dialled the FBI again this time it was a contact. "Jess? Steve. I've gone through your PR office and been given an, I'll get back to you, line."

What's the story?"

"It's about a missing cop that your guys have arrested for alleged drug smuggling, smells fishy to me. Where is she and how come a homicide detective finds herself enough time to run a drug smuggling business?"

"Name?"

Harriet Sullivan."

"Can you give me a minute?"

"Yea I'll hang on. Jane could you get me a coffee, oh and a doughnut, thanks."

"Steve.?"

"Yea I'm still here."

"It's classified under Executive Order 13526."

"You're kidding. What level?"

"Top secret under legitimate need to know."

"Are you telling me that she is a danger to the national security of the Unite States of America? Bullshit."

"Are you going ahead with it?"

"You bet we're running this story it'll be in tomorrow's edition."

"This a very prickly one Steve I would proceed with extreme caution."

"I'm always cautious Jess you know that, can you tell me anything, off the record?"

"Sorry., no can do. There's a news blackout on this one."

"Since when has drug smuggling endangered security and warranted slapping a news blackout? You know the politicians will be forced to get involved."

"Like who?"

Well for instance I don't think the governor of Utah will be too pleased."

"Still can't help you."

Ok, Ok I understand...understand your position I mean."

"I'll have a word with Jolly."

"Sure you can talk to my editor, I'll get him to call you if you want."

"Are we good?"

"No, no hard feelings, ciao."

Jessel printed off Mitch's emailed story stood up and walked to the far end of the newsroom through a swing door and along the corridor. He tapped on the door marked Arnault Jollenbeck Editor and went in.

"Arnie, Eliot Mitchell has sent in a beaut. FBI have arrested and 'disappeared' a senior homicide cop and listen to this, they've slapped a classification top secret on information on her whereabouts. This may have been the reason Mitch's fighting for his life in a hospital in Salt Lake City. I've just been told to lay off by the FBI, they might want to try leaning on you too." He handed him the email and sat down.

"What's this all about Steven?"

"We had a tip off from Salt Lake City that the police were examining cases marked as accidents, suicides and natural causes, as homicides. So we sent Mitch to find out what was happening because we knew the investigating officer was an old girlfriend of his. Now there are three attempts on her life and she gets arrested by the FBI and is spirited away. He lands up in hospital. Someone really important does not want this story to come out."

"It doesn't make any sense we're not living in a police state."

"Hell I don't know what is going on either. I've sent someone local round to her parents in Florida and Karina is going to Utah. This is a big one Arnie and we're only scratching the surface. Do you have any contacts in the FBI?"

"No no-one on a decent pay grade but I know the Chairman of the Homeland Security Committee, I'll call him. You know that feeling you've got for this story, so have I."

Harriet lay naked, floating face up inside a buoyant salt water sensory deprivation tank. The level of salt to buoyancy matched her weight completing a sense of hanging weightlessness. With no light no sound and the water set at blood temperature, all her senses were useless. She couldn't even feel the soft chord binding her wrists behind her back any more. No sense of time, space, touch, smell, sight or sound. It could have been 10 minutes it could have been an hour it was impossible to even guess. Harriet started counting and then became distracted and annoyingly lost count then gave up. It was not unpleasant. She was no stranger to contemplative therapy having practised focussed attention meditation in the Buddhist Samatha tradition. She concentrated on her breathing. As far as she knew this had never been done in such a tank before but now she didn't know if her eyes were open or closed or even whether she was awake or asleep and dreaming.

A worm of panic nibbled at her fears for the first time but she easily dismissed them. How long would they keep her here? What would she feel like when they let her out? Would she drown if she fell asleep? And yet there was no tension in her body. This was what it must have been like in the womb. She licked her lips and tasted the salt. That was once sense they couldn't take away. It was a small triumph that she clung onto like a drowning sailor holding onto a flimsy piece of flotsam. Were they monitoring her using night vision equipment? She didn't care. She wondered why Briscoe had left so abruptly, perhaps something out of their control was stirring. Maybe the PD was kicking up a fuss. She hoped that someone was kicking up a fuss. An astonishing image of Mitch in breathless detail appeared startling her. Was this the beginning of hallucinations? He was looking at her in the same preoccupied way that he did after they made love. She never knew what was going through his mind.

The image slowly disappeared leaving a ghostly imprint on her consciousness. The worm of panic appeared once more but she countered by concentrating on her breathing again and it left. She wondered what would have happened to her if she had told Briscoe about Bailey and Bailey's illegal shipments of Niobium into the States and the involvement of the Department of Defense. Maybe she would have been killed. Just another irrefutable accident that, no matter how much noise her family friends and colleagues made, it would blow over given time. An intense wave of sadness washed over her bringing a tear trickling down her cheek, a tear that she could not wipe away. She thought about all her regrets. An open Pandora's Box of memories that she would have rather forgotten flooded back adding to her isolation. Would she go insane, sectioned and incarcerated in a mental home under sedation for the rest of her life? She thought she felt her body roll turning to the left. Her shoulder was dipping or was that another trick of the senses.

She could counter it but if it was her imagination she would over compensate and roll to the right. Real panic set in. She was hyperventilating, her breath in short bursts rapidly increasing. Something was definitely happening. She was determined she wasn't going to scream. An all-consuming thought gripped her, the water entering her mouth in her nose trickling down her throat, into her lungs when she would start to cough to attempt to get rid of the water from her lungs and then she heard a voice. *'Overcome the fear, fear is the danger, fear is the enemy.'* It was her father's voice whispering to her as if he was with her in the tank knowing she was in trouble, demanding to be listened to even though it was only a whisper. Listening and breathing, then a deep breath exhaled slowly. The panic was over thanks to her father. But her memory was becoming distorted, malleable and pliant. It seemed such a long time ago but she couldn't remember getting into the tank, maybe they'd drugged her. It was getting claustrophobic reminding her of fears while caving with her father in Spencer Canyon when she was quite young and much to the disapproval of her mother.

'Everybody feels claustrophobic to some degree it's just a question of controlling fear, that's what caving is all about testing your mental strength and keeping control,' he would say.

Harriet always had enduring faith in her father's abilities and trusted him implicitly but the memory still scared her. He would always go first but it was no consolation to know that if he could squeeze through the narrow passages so could she. What would she do if he got stuck? But then they emerged as they always did into the bright daylight with fresh plant smells banishing the dank cave odours.

"Never again," she would shout at her father...until the next time. A muscular spasm shook her. Had she fallen asleep and woken up again? It was impossible to tell.

It was late and Jeff was at his desk exhausted. He had hardly seen Nancy since she had returned from Arizona. Working on Harriet's disappearance was taking up all his time.

Stokes was coming out of his office. "Hey Blackwell are you still here?"

"Same as you Serge."

"Yeah well go home and get some shut-eye I need you fresh tomorrow."

21

He knew Nancy would be in bed asleep and that he would have to quietly slip into bed. Sometimes she would turn over and he wasn't sure if he had wakened her. He took his clothes off in the dark, couldn't find his pyjamas and sat at the end of the bed. He couldn't believe that the FBI had the power to just make someone disappear. That kind of thing used to happen in South American countries like Chile. There was a gnawing feeling inside that maybe he wouldn't see Harriet again. He set his phone alarm and put it under his pillow. Nancy was lying on her back gently snoring. He started praying, not on your knees hands clasped praying but a simple communication. He prayed for Harriet's safety and for a clue, a break, something he could get his teeth into that would stop this whole thing. He slid into bed falling asleep almost immediately but the nights were always too short and before long he awoke with the vibrating phone. After a quick shower he dressed as Nancy woke and yawned.

"Didn't here you come in."

Didn't want to waken you, how are you feeling?"

"Keep feeling sick but it's not so bad. I know you're working hard Jeff," She said sitting up. "I don't mind, just find Harriet." Jeff sat on the bed and kissed her. "Did I tell you that Beth in the office started an on-line petition to release Harriet?" She said. "And it's all over Twitter with #freeharriet. The petition has reached 382,000 signatures."

"This guy Briscoe, I'm going to find him and…"

"Who?"

"Just someone I need to get a hold of. He knows where Harriet is."
He kissed her again.

"Don't take any risks I don't want you disappearing as well." She
got out of bed. "I'll make you breakfast."

Jeff shook his head. "I need to get back to the office."

It didn't take long in the early traffic to reach Police HQ and
now he was back at his desk desperately trying to probe FBI
contacts even those he hadn't spoken to for many years, calling
in previous favours to no avail. His phone rang. He ignored it at
first but it was persistent. He picked it up.

"Who…? I'll come to reception." Jeff hung up the phone and
made his way downstairs. "Donald, it's been a long time, good to
see you. Come upstairs…"

Harriet's father looked tired. "No I can't stay long I've called a
family meeting. This is a dreadful business and none of it makes
sense, does anybody know what's going on?"

"The Diner's across the road let's go over and have a coffee and I
can catch up on some breakfast."

"No, you haven't got a jacket."

"Never mind that." Jeff led him by the arm.

"Hello Jeff who's this you're arresting?" asked Jan with a smile.

"This is Harriet's father." Jeff guided Donald to the usual seat in
the corner. "Donald have some breakfast," he said.

"No just coffee."

"Full breakfast Jan…the works."

"What's happening to Sully it's all over the news?" she asked.

Jeff looked at his watch. "To be honest I'm not quite sure." She went off to get his order. He looked across the table at Donald. "This is a worrying time for all of us Donald. You know she was arrested on some trumped up charge by the FBI and squirrelled away somewhere and they're not releasing any information about her."

"How long have you been her partner?"

The question surprised Jeff. "Oh we're not really partners we were consigned murders that were linked, why?"

"Well I am going to have to take a leap of faith believing that you are the first person she would trust with her life."

"Of course we look out for each other."

"When she was in Colombia she mailed me a note." He paused and took out an envelope from his pocket and handed it to Jeff. The outer envelope with Donald's address held the unopened inner envelope with the message:

'Dad,
Please keep this safe until you hear from me. I'll explain later.
Love H
X'

"I reckon she posted it because she knew something might happen and it did."

Jeff felt the envelope recognising the shape of a memory card. "Do you know what it is?"

Donald shook his head. He leant forward and touched Jeff's arm "If you can, please tell me what's going on."

"One breakfast special Jeff, sorry for the wait guys had to make a fresh brew." Jan poured the coffee and sensing something was wrong left them.

Jeff tapped the table with his fingers and took a sip of coffee. "Sully is a remarkable cop. She uncovered the Borisov group of imported contract killers from Belarus that have been responsible for a large number of deaths in Utah including your brother. That's just the tip of the iceberg. It's very complicated but one thing's for sure if anything happens to Sully while she's in the custody of the FBI, I won't rest until those responsible are caught and punished. Have you heard anything from Frank Calderwood?"

"He's lodged the papers with the court and he has also made a formal complaint to the Office of the Inspector General who have the authority to investigate actions taken by FBI employees but this could all take a great deal of ..." Donald's phone rang out. "Hello Matti."

"Where are you?"

"I'm with Jeff just now, we're in a diner near the police HQ."

"Mitch is seriously ill. He fell or was pushed down a flight of stairs.

"When?"

"Yesterday, I've just had a reporter at the door. Will you tell Jeff?"

"Oh dear." He rang off and put the phone back in his pocket. "Mitch is seriously ill in hospital. He filed a story with the Washington Post. One of their reporters called at the house wanting a quote about Harriet's arrest. It's going to be in tomorrow's edition." He touched the envelope on the table. "I hope this helps it must have been important for Harriet to post it to me."

22

"*They will kill me.*"

"*They will not know, of course if you prefer Pedrinhas Prison…It's a jungle…be-headings, male rape, riots, turf wars, the wardens have no control.*"

"*I didn't know they killed Miguel. Ok 70% of Niobium production is exported without the correct documentation to America. It is listed as fertilizer and travels in sealed containers by ship. It's unloaded at the container terminal in Port of Los Angeles San Pedro after that I don't know.*"

"*The US has the most efficient and rigorous import controls in the world how can anyone possibly smuggle in such huge amounts of Niobium?*"

"*You don't know? Bailey and Bailey have very influential friends in Washington. How else would it be possible?*"

"*Influential friends, who? Which department?*"

"*Defense.*"

"*Do you have a name?*"

"*That's all I know.*"

Chief Ross McLeod stopped the recording and looked Grainger Stokes and Jeff. "This was posted to Sullivan's father and he gave it to you?"

"Unopened."

"Let me just get this straight. Bailey and Bailey organised the killing of the CEO of this Brazilian company, bought it over and appointed one of their own to smuggle this mineral into the US with the full knowledge and blessing of someone in the Defense Department. Have I missed anything out? Grainger what do you make of this? Why can't we produce our own Niobium?" asked the Chief.

"We have no deposits of the rare earth mineral all we can do is import and retrieve the mineral from scrap. This confirms Harriet's theory and we now have a lead but we're short on evidence. The word of a crooked CEO doesn't count for much. But where do we go from here Chief this is way out of our jurisdiction. Who can we trust in the FBI to release this information to? They can't even police themselves. Do you know that in the FBI out of over 5,000 allegations of misconduct received internally over a two year period and investigated 74% were placed in the zero file, that's no further action will be taken. They're untouchable. Of course it all depends on how high up within the FBI these decisions were taken or agreed," said Grainger.

"SACS, Chief of Staff, Associate Deputy Director, Deputy Director and hell knows maybe the Director himself," said the Chief

"What about the Office of the Director of National Intelligence that heads the US Intelligence Community?" asked Grainger.

The Chief wiped the sweat from his brow with a tissue and shook his head. "There are sixteen members of the US Intelligence community, eight of them report directly to the Defense Department. So what's left? CIA, Homeland Security, Justice Department, Energy Department and the Treasury department. Take your pick."

"There is the State Department's Bureau of Intelligence and

Research."

"No good they supply information to diplomats that shapes foreign policy. I think it has to be the CIA." There was a silence in the office. "You look doubtful Grainger."

"The CIA has had a very chequered and murky past with rogue operatives and clandestine operations that probably even the President doesn't know about."

"They've gone through a major reorganization and restructuring." Jeff's phone rang. He looked at it and held up his hand "Yes transfer him, Hello Brian?"

"Is Detective Sullivan there

"I'm afraid not, she's off for a few days I'm her partner we work together. I know about your brother Jackson I'm sorry to hear about his death."

Well I need to talk to her, it's really important.

"Take your time."

"I'm really risking my neck, you don't understand how dangerous this whole thing is."

"Dangerous, how is it dangerous?"

They'd kill me if they knew I was talking to you. My brother worked for them."

Yes I knew he worked for Universal Defence and Development Contractors Corporation"

"Do you know what he did?"

"No I don't know what he did, we have a job to do Brian but thank you for the warning, can you be more specific?"

"You have to be really careful."

"Careful in what way? He rang off. That was a strange call. We know that this company UDDC researches and manufactures equipment for the Department of Defense and in the process uses large amounts of Niobium. It's primarily for experimental next generation jet engines. They also use Tantalum in the production of early design quantum computing. And it seems they are also under contract to the FBI. I wonder if Jackson was going to blow the whistle."

The Chief's phone rang out. He picked it up. "Yes?"

"A reporter wants to speak to you her name is Karina…"

"Do your job fob her off, can't comment during live investigations, the usual bullshit."

"She's from the Washington Post.

"Washington Post? Damn give her a coffee I'll be down shortly. Grainger who was Sullivan's arresting officer?"

"It was Special Agent George Briscoe."

"Can you check to see if he's in-house or contract? Just an idea."

Harriet was sweating. There was a smell that was familiar, pungent and clinical it was a mix from more than one source yet unmistakeably singular like a vet or a dentist surgery. Something flickered above her buzzing and clicking resembling a faulty starter switch failing to ionize a fluorescent tube. Perhaps its familiarity was causing Harriet to resist, pushing the memory further into the reaches of her consciousness.

"Hello Harriet."

The soft unmistakeable voice of Dr Henry Speed momentarily stopped her shallow breathing. The arcing tube light came on silhouetting his head. He was wearing protective glasses, a face mask and his usual deodorant that she had always detested. She tried to speak but couldn't. She tried to move, to blink, to turn her head anything that would give her hope but she couldn't. She just felt the cold slab underneath cooling her naked body, still she could not shiver. She tried to rationalize. Was it the returning nightmare or was it real?

"I don't usually make a habit of speaking to my customers but for you I'll make an exception. You really are a good looking woman with, I have to say, a beautiful body and I particularly like the butterfly tattoo on your hip. Such a waste. You know I don't like open eyes but yours are lovely."

He leaned forward. She felt his lips touching hers and smelled his breath. This wasn't the same as in her dream.

"You can be quite cold and distant. I can't quite understand where we got off on the wrong foot. However I have a job to do, a full autopsy, I think. We have to find out how you died, natural causes most likely. I wonder how much your brain weighs. Let's see shall we?"

Speed picked something up. Harriet saw the glint of a large sharp surgical saw in one hand and a scalpel in the other. She tried to scream but all she could hear was the metallic contact of the scalpel running along the teeth of the blade and then everything went black.

Harriet regained consciousness sensing a trace of disinfectant. She opened her eyes. Above her on the ceiling was what looked like a mirror image of her lying naked on a crisp starched white sheet. She stared at it in horror, numbed by the vision of a limbless body. Her legs and arms had been removed with just stitches remaining to close the wound. Tears welled and ran down her impassive cheeks. Inside there was revulsion, frustration, anger and then futility. It hadn't been a nightmare after all it was real, but she felt no pain, not even the slightest ache. Surely after surgery like that no matter how strong the drugs were, there would be something, an indication of the amputation. An inner strength refused to believe what had happened she closed her eyes unable to watch her limbless torso anymore.

"How is she reacting?" Briscoe and Speed were looking through a two way mirror.

"Hard to tell with Pancuronium," replied Speed. "It's a neuromuscular-blocking drug normally used by anaesthetists and in euthanasia and in some states in the country for executions. But I think I can see a tear on her cheek. You know it's a very fine line getting the balance right, too much and she's dead or at best needing a respirator, too little and she would have enough muscular capability to discover what happened. You have an hour before the drug starts wearing off. That large pasted photo-shopped image under glass on the ceiling is amazingly realistic."

"We're not animals, there is a purpose to all of this and it's not sadism. I spent three tours of duty in Afghanistan with a Psyops unit, you have to be inventive. She'll tell us anything we want to know now. Let's get her into the other room."

Harriet was struggling with her emotions when she heard her father's voice again.

'It's all about testing your mental strength and keeping control of fear.'

She was vaguely aware of movement and opened her eyes. A drip tube from a suspended plastic bag above her swung from side to side. The corridor ceiling with flat panels of strip-lights passed over her then the frame of a doorway into a room.

Briscoe appeared and looked down at her. He shone a light into her eyes and her pupils retracted. He looked at his watch and studied her without speaking for several minutes.

"Harriet I know you can hear me and you should be able to talk now. You're limbs have been removed. You will not be able to walk or do anything for yourself for the rest of your life without help. You have been given a dose of a muscular paralysis drug known as Pancuronium. An overdose is fatal." He pointed to the plastic bag. "This contains Pancuronium. There is a small tap here that will release the drug if you wish and end your life painlessly. In return I need some information. Speculation can be dealt with, that's not a problem. Evidence on the other hand is much more difficult to negate. According to Flavio you have a recording of Señor Cabral being shall we say a little indiscreet. Ah you wouldn't have heard he had an unfortunate accident at the mine, they are such dangerous places, a cave in I believe. Now, where is the recording?"

Harriet was in shock. She could still see the image of herself lying on the bed. The idea that anyone could be so callous and cruel was beyond comprehension. She closed her eyes "I posted it to my Father in Florida."

"Thank you Harriet, now that wasn't too difficult was it?"

She opened her eyes. He was smiling at her. "Do it now and get it over with," she said.

"Not quite there yet," he said. How far up the chain did you get?"

"Someone in the defense department, that's all. Please just do it."

"That won't be necessary." He said winding the tube round the bag. He picked up her limp arms by the wrist for her to see. "It wasn't connected, smoke and mirrors. Now I have to say goodbye Harriet and thank you."

Speed picked up a syringe and tapped the air from it.

"You can't possibly get away with this."

"This is a drug that will put you to sleep and erase your recent memory. You will have no recollection of the sensory deprivation tank or your short spell in the morgue with me or my friend Mr Briscoe, bon voyage."

Harriet drifted off to sleep.

"Will her memory loss be permanent?" asked Briscoe.

"That's what I'm told but it's hard to say, but for how long... is anybody's guess. This is still an experimental drug tested on captured terrorists after interrogation so that they wouldn't remember any, shall we say persuasive techniques."

"Well we have to release her, the pressure is building. On-line petitions, lobbying Senators and congressmen and the press are spending a great deal of time and money trying to find her. We can't take the risk that her memory will return let's give her a few days or so and find an unfortunate accident waiting for the young lady."

23

"Donald its Jeff. Harriet's been released by the FBI. She's at the University Hospital."

He was making his way through the corridors of the Neuropsychiatric Institute, Chipeta Way, more like a five star hotel than a hospital.

"Thank God, what happened?"

"They said she's had a nervous breakdown."

"Where are you?"

"I'm at the hospital now."

"Have you seen her? Is she Ok?"

"I haven't seen her yet. All the charges have been dropped."

"The FBI came to our house looking for the envelope. They could only have known that we had it from Harriet herself. I told them we didn't have it and they were not welcome here."

"Don't worry about it they won't be showing up here looking for it. No harm done Donald, I'll call you later when I see her."

Jeff flashed his badge at the police guard outside Harriet's room and entered. The room was small and simply furnished. Light came streaming through a single curtain-less window illuminating a full sized bed containing Harriet. She was lying motionless with her eyes closed. The lack of colour in her face may have been caused by the ambient light or it could have been the result of her breakdown. Jeff walked past the shower and toilet noticing that a third of the door had been cut down at an angle allowing some privacy for a patient. The lights were recessed and there was no chair only a simple bedside cabinet. He sat on the edge of the bed and reached out touching her hand. She opened her eyes and turned her head towards him. The weary smile said it all.

Jeff squeezed her hand. "Are you Ok? I've just spoken to your Dad he knows you're here."

"Hello Jeff. I don't know what they gave me but I'm enjoying it. Where am I and how did I get here?"

"The FBI took you here in an ambulance. You had been arrested by them and held for almost a week. All charges have been dropped. I have a statement from them released to the press." He took out his phone and looked at her. "We can do this later if you want."

"No it's Ok, carry on."

'Ms Sullivan has been released by the FBI and after extensive and thorough investigations no charges will be brought. She has suffered a nervous breakdown while in custody and has been taken to the Neuropsychiatric Institute, Chipeta Way for examination and treatment. We would like to affirm that the FBI was not in any way responsible for her unfortunate condition.'

Harriet closed her eyes and gripped his hand. "Jeff I don't remember anything." A tear slowly made its way down her cheek.

"You will, don't worry you will. You're father gave me the flash drive you posted to him from Colombia with the Señor Cabral interview. The FBI paid Donald a visit which raises the certainty that the only way they could have known that you're father had the memory card was from you. Anyway they were too late.

Cabral is dead by the way, mining accident it seems."

"Stop. Jeff I don't know what you're talking about."

"I'm going too fast I brought you a copy of this mornings' Washington Post. You're on the front page. Incidentally the Doctors have told me that there are possible residues of a drug that can impair memory in your bloodstream but they're not 100% convinced they want to do more tests. If it is true there doesn't appear to be an anti-dote as such, yet."

"I don't understand. Jeff I want to get out of here."

"What can you remember?"

"It's like I've had a long sleep. When I try to remember I get this very vague feeling of apprehension and…I can't think."

There was a tap at the door. Harriet saw her lawyer Frank Calderwood through a pane of glass on the door and beckoned him in.

"Hi Harriet you're looking a lot better than I expected."

"I'm fine. This is a colleague of mine Jeff, my lawyer Frank."

"Harriet the Doctors tell me that you have lost a big chunk of your short term memory."

"Yes."

"Ok do you feel strong enough for some bad news."

"Yes."

Your Uncle Lawrence is dead."

"Oh, I didn't really know him that well, poor Dad."

"Well these are the papers for you to sign should you wish to pursue the FBI for damages and I need you to sign confirmation of receipt of the contents of your Uncles bequest."

"Bequest what bequest, you mean some money?"

"I've never shocked the same person twice over a will. Brace yourself Harriet. Under the terms of the will Lawrence left you $5m, a string of racehorses, a franchise of stores selling guns and an apartment in the city." He put a foolscap envelope on the bed. "The details are all in there. If there's anything you need, get in touch."

"Thanks Frank." Harriet waited until he had left. "Get me my clothes Jeff and let's get the hell out of here."

"Where do you want to go?"

"Home. I need to see something familiar."

Jeff started the car and left the Hospital grounds. "I'm afraid I have more bad news Harriet." He hesitated.

"Go for it."

"Mitch is in hospital on the critical list. He was found at the bottom of a flight of stairs in a bad way. I'm sorry."

"Mitch? How? Why?"

Harriet listened as Jeff explained what had happened as they travelled home. He looked over occasionally to see she was taking it well if looking perpetually puzzled.

"Have you read the Post?" The Secretary of State for Defense Dekker Stadler grunted as he and his aide entered the Oval Office. President Alvera Yolanda looked over her reading glasses at the pair as they entered. Already seated was Under Secretary of Defense for Acquisitions, technology and logistics, Ethan Tyler, FBI Director Gary Hunt and Director of the CIA Michael Holman. Papers were uncharacteristically scattered across the coffee table separating the two sofas with the Washington Post on top. President Yolanda's phone rang as she gestured for them to sit then swivelled her chair to look out the window. The men nodded to each and sat down. Holman helped himself to a coffee from the silver tray and looked questioningly at Hunt who shrugged. Portraits of George Washington and Abraham Lincoln looked down.

"Ok thanks for that Tom." she put the phone down. "Morning gentlemen," she said crossing the room and sitting down. "Garry, Mike, what the heck is going on in Utah?"

"There's been a foul up." Holman put down the cup. "Clive Bailey the CEO of Bailey and Bailey and Red Cutler who owns Universal Defence and Development Contractors Corporation have overstepped the mark in their enthusiasm to corner the market on rare minerals. We did not give them carte blanche and unfortunately their actions have endangered our supply and may lead back to this office."

"Mike I was expressly told that these corporations were vital to the future well-being of America and that they should be given a free hand to manage the mining resources buying into critically important producers of these minerals so I'm asking once more what the hell is going on in Utah?"

FBI Director Gary Hunt cleared his throat. "Ma'am Niobium is a very special metal it is absolutely essential for development across the board. It has a highly significant mineral for military applications, next generation computers, aeronautics, we simply couldn't function without this metal. In Salt Lake City Police Department there is a very clever and tenacious homicide Detective called Harriet Sullivan who has been following the trail on a series of sudden deaths that we now know to be murder."

"What? How many?"

"We don't know exactly, low double figures. These two CEO's brought in hired contractors that we thought were for defense. It turns out they were being used as hit men with a brief to make the killings look accidental. We found out about them when Sullivan tipped us off."

"Why can't we arrest these guys and shut their companies down?"

They both looked at Ethan Tyler. "Well Ma'am our rare earth minerals were almost exhausted before these two companies stepped in and it is now secure for the long term future…"

"…At a cost."

"Yes Ma'am unknown to us. However we are by no means out of the woods due to severe restrictions imposed by nationally owned producers abroad, this is effectively stopping some of the rarer minerals being sold on the open market."

"Our only option is to mitigate any potential damage to the Presidency by these two companies," said Hunt.

"Damn the presidency gentlemen, this is extremely important. How complicit are the security services in what went on?"

Hunt sighed. "Some of our agents were perhaps overzealous in protecting the free flow of rare minerals and as a result may have colluded with the companies mentioned. One group of agents in particular contracted to the FBI. It is a very delicate situation. With Niobium for example, we are now secure reserve holders."

"How vulnerable are you in all of this Decker?" asked the President.

"If the Bailey's and Cutler went public my position would be untenable and the public and the press could never be sure that you weren't in some way implicated it would probably bring down the government."

President Alvera Yolanda sighed. "These FBI contractors...get their badges and kick them off the force. Gentlemen I've made a decision I hope I'm not going to regret."

24

Bonneville Flats was covered with a winter layer of water that, in the stillness was like an immaculately polished mirror. A very fine haze on the horizon fused reality with reflection unable to define where one ended and the other began. A Bell 525 Relentless appeared in the cloudless sky in synchrony with its perfect inverted image below, heading for a mile long spit of land piercing deep into the salt flats. A mirror window clad dodecahedra structure with a slate grey helipad on the roof stood sentinel at the tip of the sand-spit. The helicopter landed and while the blades were still turning four armed men appeared from it followed by a single passenger who was shepherded inside. Red Cutler the CEO of Universal Defence and Development Contractors Corporation descended a spiral staircase to find a large glass decagonal table surrounded by Philippe Starck Ghost chairs. Clive Bailey was in a heated conversation with his brother Maurice and stopped as Cutler approached the table.

"What a wonderful view," said Cutler.

Clive Bailey cleared his throat. "We're in deep trouble. Now that the cat is well and truly out of the bag, the President is trying to distance the presidency from our companies. Latest is they don't quite know what to do with us. As I see it we have to have a contingency plan that will persuade the Government to find an equitable solution."

"Breath taking," Cutler said still standing, gazing out.

"Well we could threaten to sell the companies to let's say to the Chinese for example. Criminal liability doesn't preclude ownership of a company and as owners of companies with no shareholders we can do what we like with them."

"They might just seize the businesses," said his brother.

"And risk a full blown disclosure to the press? Red you don't seem to be interested in the possibility that we are all going to spend the rest of our lives in jail."

"Oh but I do, I do. I've always been blessed with a sense of fatalism. Our lives are preordained from conception to death mapped out in finite detail we are merely passengers in our own bodies. Besides that," He paused for effect. "I've got cancer and the Doc has given me a few months at best. So in three words, I don't care. My family are all taken care of with offshore trusts that are untouchable even if they were found."

"Why did you bother coming?" asked Clive.

"I came because I care about my employees, sentimental I know. I want to try and ensure the business carries on in one form or another."

"So what would you suggest?"

"Let's look at the options. We could put our hands up and say sorry we're bad guys don't lock us up and throw away the key. We could disappear, plastic surgery new identity, neutral country that's not going to kick us out. Or we could have a big powwow with the various Government departments to try for a minimum security prison like Lone Peak, and Promontory."

Clive wagged his finger. "For the rest of our lives, no thanks. What proof does SLCPD have?"

Red sat down at the table. "They have a tape of the manager in Brazil confessing to illegally exporting Niobium into the States."

"Is there any evidential link between the contractors and us?"

Red poured himself a glass of water. "I don't think so but this woman detective, what's her name, Sullivan, was investigating sudden deaths but she is in no position to carry on with that inquiry."

"Well then," said Clive. "I would suggest a cessation and forensic clean-out of all illegal operations, a meeting with Decker and a maximum damage limitation exercise underway. Red you have financial connections to some influential newspapers. Get them on the case rubbishing the SLC police investigation."

"Ok sounds like a plan, I'll do that but there is another problem, The Brazilian Government is not too pleased about us illegally shipping out the Niobium."

"Come on Red, We're talking Brazil here, somebody gets paid, easy."

"What's the last thing you remember?"

Harriet's Doctor, Peter with legs crossed leaned back in his chair looking over his reading glasses at her. He had been there when Harriet first came into the world, watched her grow, treated a few minor ailments and then lost touch principally because he was not needed.

"A party. I was at a party, I can't think why, I'm not all that keen on parties. It must have been a special occasion."

Peter smiled. This was the brain of a detective piecing clues together.

"Somebodies birthday, no. There were people there from the PD. Ha, New Year's Eve. It was New Year's Eve, yes! That's my last memory. Maybe I had a little too much to drink."

"Is that deduction or memory?"

She smiled. "A bit of both."

"Physically there is nothing wrong with you. I don't think there is any need for you to worry. Go on holiday Harriet, not Brazil, somewhere nice, Florida maybe, spend time with your Mum and Dad."

"Jeff, what are you doing?" The office was unusually quiet.

"Sully I didn't expect to see you here. Um, you haven't seen Stokes yet."

"No I just got here. What's going on?"

"There's been a major reorganisation. Homicide is being split up, new people coming in from out of State."

"What?"

"I've been transferred to Ogden. Stokes is going to Provo. The cases are being reassigned to the new boys."

"Just a minute," she said walking towards the Sergeant's Stokes office. "Don't go anywhere just yet." She opened the door to see Stokes emptying his desk into a cardboard box. She knocked on the open door but he ignored her. "Grainger...Grainger. Look somehow I get the feeling this is all my fault. If it is I'm sorry. Where's my badge? I still work here don't I? Look just because I've a memory gap that doesn't change who I am. Do I still have a case? Grainger!"

"Not my call now. It's over Sully your badge has been taken away, you don't work here anymore, and for that matter neither do I. I'm sorry. You shouldn't even be in the building."

Harriet stepped inside and slammed the door shut with a bang making Stokes jump. "Listen to me Sergeant Grainger Stokes

I know I was working on something important. I know the FBI kidnapped me probably to get some information and then drugged me so that I wouldn't remember. Now I don't care if I get kicked out or not I'm not walking away from this case."

"Go home Harriet you won't get near any of the files, they're all in a safe in the chiefs' office. Oh and by the way we have a new Chief. If you want my advice I think you should see a therapist."

Harriet left him packing his belongings and walked over to Jeff's desk. He powered down his computer and turned to look at her folding his arms, and wearing a smile. She smiled back and gave him a hug. "My first and last case."

"I heard you shouting at Stokes," he said picking up his box. "Oh, I think you should say goodbye to Ben, he's staying put. Nancy's back, come round tonight, have dinner with us." He made a fake salute and left.

Harriet watched him leave just as the phone on her desk started to ring. She rushed over and picked it up. "Hello?"

"Is that Detective Sullivan?"

"Yes?"

"This is Brian Irving we need to meet."

"I'm sorry who?"

"My brother Jackson was killed."

"Oh yes," she lied. "Can we meet at Jan's Diner across from HQ say in about thirty minutes?"

"Ok."

Harriet hurried along to IT forensics but Ben wasn't there. "Damn, damn, damn," she said kicking a desk.

"Hey leave my desk alone," he said coming in. "What are you playing at...kicking my best friend."

"Ben I'm so pleased to see you, how come you survived the cull?"

"I had prior knowledge. How are you Sully?"

"Don't ask. I understand all the files of my case are locked up."

"Maybe…maybe not," he smiled.

"What do you mean?"

"Well they have a copy of everything I had…a copy."

"Ben if you were unattached I'd kiss you." Harriet looked at her watch. "Would you settle for a coffee?"

"I'm really up to the eyes. Look it's already on this memory stick, here."

She put it into her bag. "Please? I'm meeting someone in the Diner and I don't have a clue who he is or what he wants."

Gleb Durchenko was tired of the cat and mouse constantly on the go moving from one cheap motel to another. He needed to leave. Go to a country where his talents would be used and rewarded but he was being strung along. He stopped the red dust covered pick-up on a track inside Arches National Park, switched off the engine and got out. A jet 35,000 feet up crossed the deep blue sky leaving a white vapour trail. He took out his phone and slipped it under his seat. He put a handgun and water in a small backpack and slung it over his shoulder. Then he picked up a rifle with a telescopic sight and put it over his shoulder. It didn't take him long to climb the three hundred feet up the side of Devils' Canyon where he chose a spot next to Double O Arch giving him a clear view of the valley floor. He was always cautious, always minimizing any possible unforeseen event, that's why he was still alive. He had received a text ordering a meeting and had chosen this remote location to give him an advantage should it be a trap. He knew they would locate him through his phone. A pair of Coopers' Hawks flew over his head calling and surprised he reached for his rifle. They swooped downhill and disappeared from sight just as the tell-tale column of dust signalled the presence of an approaching vehicle. Durchenko lifted his rifle resting it on one knee and put his eye to the scope. It looked like it carried only one person, the driver. As it got closer the cross hairs focussed revealing George Briscoe at the wheel. Briscoe pulled up next to the pickup and got out holding an envelope. He walked to the truck and looked in the open window. He checked the position on his mobile and sure enough this is where the signal came from.

"Durchenko!" Briscoe's call echoed round the canyon. Then he saw him walking down the hill towards him until they were face to face. "Always suspicious," he said.

"Can't be too careful. I have to get the hell out of this country. My time here is over I'm leaving the US."

"Of course and we will help you do just that but there is one last job. One last piece of tidying up to do."

"Why can't you do it?"

Briscoe ignored the question and handed him the envelope. Durchenko opened it and snorted.

"Why did you not finish her off when you had her?"

"It wasn't possible, we had to let her go. It has to be suicide or an accident I don't care which, a clean killing. I want her dead before she knows it."

"And when it's done?"

"I can have you on a cargo jet to Bolivia where you can go on to anywhere you want."

"I don't like it. There's something about this policewoman. We've tried to kill her twice and you tried in Brazil."

"Fourth time lucky then."

25

Ben and Harriet entered the Diner.

Jan rushed over and gave her a hug. "Are you alright we've all been worried about you."

Harriet smiled. "I'm fine now." She looked round the Diner. "Is there anyone here who is not a regular?" Jan nodded towards a young man who was texting. Harriet looked at Ben and they went over. "Brian?" He nodded awkwardly. They both shook Brian's hand and sat down as Jan re-appeared. "Two coffees please."

"Ahem," said Ben clearing his throat. "Do you have any of that wonderfully creamy gateaux left from yesterday?"

"Sure have, Ben. You're very pale and putting on weight, you need to get out more."

"Tell me about it."

She looked at Brian and topped up his coffee and went off looking for another cup to refill.

"You were right about Jackson, he was killed."

"Hold on, tell you what why don't you start at the beginning?" she said.

Ben took out his phone pressed record and set it on the table.

"Jackson was a procurement officer in UDDC and discovered

that a shipment of Niobium he purchased had been imported illegally. He found documentation miss-describing the contents on the entry waybill and brought it to the attention of the Head of Procurement. He was told there must have been an error in the paper work and to ignore it. I work in accounts in Bailey and Bailey International Commodities Broker Incorporated and when he told me this, I did a database check and discovered he was right. I checked my computer and found an email from him saying he was sorry, that he couldn't go on. Then the police came to the house and told us that Jackson had thrown himself off a building. I read the email again and it just wasn't convincing. We were identical twins. There is a bond, a connection between twins. If he had been suicidal I would have known about it. My line manager found out that I had been poking around the company server and gave me a warning."

"What kind of warning, what did he say?"

Brian's looked around the diner nervously. "He took me into his office and put his hand on my shoulder and whispered into my ear, 'You don't want to end up like your brother now do you? Live and let live Brian, let me give you a piece of advice. Keep your head down and just do the job, that's good advice, remember it.' I was stunned. He was practically admitting that Jackson had been murdered and was using that to threaten me. I decided that I couldn't just go on as if nothing was wrong so I downloaded a worm from the internet at home, put it on a memory stick and plugged it into my office computer. It lay dormant until I got home. Going through a VPN for anonymity I woke it and it started searching and sending me all kinds of files." He looked at them both with eyes wide open.

"Did you find what you were looking for?" asked Harriet gently.

"Everything. Shipments, dates, ports, tonnages, coded names with an index of codes."

"Brazil?"

"Brazil, Tanzania, Australia, Zambia, Canada, Malawi and it's being illegally brought into the country refined and stockpiled in an old disused open cast mine in Arizona that's very heavily guarded. Trucks are emptying their loads round the clock…it's a huge operation. Not only that I also have…"

"…Ok what's wrong with the coffee and Ben you haven't even touched your cake."

"Sorry Jan could we have some fresh coffee and put it on my tab. Go on Brian."

"I also managed to intercept the company secure email client. The emails are detailed conversations between government Defense Department employees and the company. Niobium is an extremely important mineral considered 'strategic and critical' by the US Government and 'essential for national security and industry.' In relation to the 2008's Government's stockpile of Niobium in the Defense National Stockpile Center (DNSC) the Government said that the US's Niobium stock had been depleted and that further sales would be discontinued. That's how serious it was. Niobium is so important it's not even traded on the open commodities market it's sold directly to manufactures. Niobium producers are regulating the price by controlling output to ensure stability. At the moment it's at $80 a kilo. Baileys plan to restrict production and force up their prices and there is absolutely nothing anyone can do about it because it's a free market."

"Do you have a record of all of this?"

"Gigabytes of the stuff…to be honest there's so much of it I've only scratched the surface."

"Could we have it?"

Brian reached into his pocket and brought out an external hard drive. He took a menu from the holder and covering the drive slid it across the table. "That's the only copy. Be careful how it's used it wouldn't take long for them to figure out it was me. Don't go sending it to Wikileaks for example I'd be dead within the hour. Listen I have to go." He got up and paused. "This is for Jackson...good luck."

Ben let his breath out as if he had only just started to breathe again. "This is dynamite. If any of these jokers know you have this stuff, well goes without saying."

"I know. Ben I only understand patches of this investigation. I'm going to spend the rest of the day going through the case notes you gave me before I look at this. I don't like the idea of being on my own at home, I'll find somewhere else."

"Do you want me to work on the drive?"

"No, if you get caught that could be the end of your career, but thanks anyway. I guess I'm the last one standing."

Harriet's cab pulled up outside the gun store. She looked out of the window at the sign that read Sullivan's and sighed. She hated guns but there was too much at stake for her to fail now. She asked the driver to wait and went in. This was the first time she had been in one and was surprised to be met by the smell of leather and gun oil. The man behind the counter studied her as she approached wiping his hands on a blue smock. He was a small man partially balding with hair coming out of his ears and nostrils, probably in his fifties and wearing a pair of small round glasses perched on his nose. He could have been a bank clerk or a chemist but here he was selling death. She looked down at the cased handguns laid out for inspection below the glass. "How many people would die with these guns she was looking at," she mused.

"How can I help you today ma'am," he said with a forced smile.

"I'd like to buy a handgun, a Glock 22 Standard .40 Smith and

Wesson 4.49 inch 15+1 w/FS Poly Grip Black and a box of ammunition with three spare clips."

Surprised that Harriet knew exactly what she wanted he took the boxed Glock and the ammo from a shelf and put it on the counter "I'll have to do a BCI check, are you Ok with that?"

"That won't be necessary I'm your new boss, Harriet Sullivan, Lawrence was my uncle and since I own all of the Sullivan Gun Stores I guess I own all these guns legally anyway a BCI check won't be required I also work for the police department."

"Yes Ma'am, sorry I didn't recognise you. That'll be $650. How would you like to pay?"

"You can put it on my tab. What's your name?"

"Mo, Mo Barclay."

"Good work Mo, glad to see you're on the ball."

Uncle Lawrence's apartment was in a very expensive part of the city's business centre. She looked at the nameplates on the entry pad and spotted Sullivan but pressed the tab below with concierge written on it. She looked up at the security camera and smiled. The door buzzed and opened. The concierge was a portly woman with a limp.

She smiled at Harriet. "Can I help you?"

"I'm Lawrence Sullivan's niece. He left the apartment to me in his will and I don't have a key."

"I'm Mrs Cotton. I'm so sorry, I heard about his unfortunate accident. I was wondering what was going to happen to his apartment. I hope you don't mind can I see some ID?"

Harriet looked for her driving licence while Mrs Cotton fetched the key from behind a desk.

"That's fine dear there's the key. I hope you have a nice stay it's the penthouse at the top. Swipe the card in the elevator and it will take you directly to your apartment."

Harriet entered the elevator just as her phone buzzed. "Hi Jeff."

"Nancy is asking if you'd like to come for a meal."

"I can't tonight I've got a lot of work to get through, how about tomorrow?"

"I'll tell her. Everything Ok? It sounds like you're in a confined space."

"Yes I'm fine I'm in an elevator, see you tomorrow."

The door opened and Harriet walked straight into the spacious apartment. There was a monochromatic theme to the décor and furnishing with white carpets, white walls, a black circular glass coffee table in front of a Georgian style Carrera marble fireplace and a white sofa with grey striped cushions. Above was a mounted LED television and below the mantelpiece another smaller TV that came alive with a movement sensor. It showed a realistic video of a coal and log fire complete with sounds of burning wood. The dining room had black sculpted chairs around a white glazed table. The kitchen next to it continued the theme with white panelled cupboards and black marble worktops. Satin chrome dishwasher, washing machine and fridge freezer completed the effect. In the bedroom a black chest of drawers sat next to a large window with expansive views of Capitol Hill. En suite was a wide door-less walk-in bathroom with a shower sink and bath all in white. She went into the kitchen, opened the fridge took out a bottle of juice then went through to the sitting room and sat down on the sofa next to the coffee table. There were a couple of remote controls and a keyboard. She switched on the television and searched source, finding computer mode. Up came a login page. She sat back on the sofa and sipped the juice.

"Ok," she said out loud, "I'm Lawrence and I know that I am going to leave all of this to you dear Harriet, so why do I need a password? To stop just anybody poking around after I'm gone of course. M...m where does that leave me. It's a word that only you would think of dummy. No...surely not." She typed Harriet and pressed enter. Nothing happened. "Come on. Don't be stupid I can't make it too easy, anybody could twig." She tried harr13t and it opened to reveal an image of one of Lawrence's race horses. Harriet stood up and punched the air. She sat down in surprise as her Uncle appeared on the screen.

"Hello Harriet, I hope you've got over the shock of your inheritance. There are only two passwords that will open this computer so I know it's you. Frank told me that there was a break in at his office and nothing was stolen. I can tell you that spooked me and I can't really explain why. So I decided to make final arrangements just in case. There is a safe behind this monitor and if you press #632549 on the keyboard the monitor will swing out and open the door of the safe. I won't tell you what's inside, I want it to be a surprise. Everything in the apartment is yours. In the wardrobe you'll find Lorraine's clothes, I kept them all these years, couldn't bear to throw them away. Lorraine was your age when she died. She was very stylish and I would be pleased if you had a use for them but don't feel honour bound. I've explained in my letter to you the reason why I took an interest in your progress from a distance. You were the daughter I never had and I'm very proud that you have achieved so much without a helping hand from anybody. I know I've given you many things and it must be said, it has given me a great deal of pleasure but there is one last thing I want to give you...some advice. Never give up. Keep fighting for all those people who for one reason or another are not as strong or as clever as you are. The ones that are ridden roughshod over who don't have access to clever lawyers. And Harriet find someone nice...get married... have kids. Goodbye Harriet and God bless."

Harriet sat there stunned with a tear on her cheek. She pressed the number and the monitor moved opening the safe. There were two metal boxes she took one out and opened it. It was full of fifty dollar bills. There must have been around a hundred thousand dollars. In the other box was Lorraine's' jewellery, gold, diamond rings, earrings, necklaces and gold coins. She took two thousand dollars and put everything back closing the door and repositioned the TV. She picked up the keyboard, found a slot for Ben's memory card and plugged it in. Immediately all the folders and files appeared. Ben had listed them chronologically which helped, so she started at the beginning. She clicked on photographs of a green car on a trailer at various angles with someone inside.

There was a report in the folder, her report. She shook her head in frustration at not remembering any of it. She read it as if for the first time and anger replaced frustration. The hours passed quickly as she watched the images, read the reports, attempts on her life, how her uncle died, contractors imported from Belorussia, killings faked as accidents or suicides, the mine in Brazil, it was all incredible. Then she had a brief flashback, it was a face peering down at her. She closed her eyes, she had been expecting something like that but it still gave her a shock. The face, it was familiar...Dr Speed. Speed and Simmons, Simmons and Speed. The flimsy autopsy that found nothing. She looked at her watch, it was after midnight. Simmons might still be in the morgue. What she had been pouring over was all beginning to be slightly familiar, the mental memory block was lifting.

26

Harriet looked at the entry keypad blankly, closed her eyes and tried to block her thoughts except for the universal code that would open any SLCPD door. Her fingers raised and punched the key pad. No. 'It's very close.' She thought. She tried again, nothing. She was worried there might be three attempts and then a lockout. She pressed the keys once more. It buzzed and opened. There was never anybody about at night in the building, no guards, nothing. Who would want to break into a morgue? She entered the room and shivered, it was cold. She ran her fingers across the marble slab and felt the veins created with impurities swirling randomly. She scanned the labels of the drawers and her heart skipped a beat when she saw the name plate, SIMMONS. She pulled open the drawer, hesitated and unzipped the body bag. A ghostly pale face with closed eyes lay there. She touched the face, it was very cold.

There was no DNA apart from Simmons in the car so someone wanting to kill him must have been outside the car. That means that there was a limited area exposed to the killer. She turned his face away from her and search his neck looking carefully inside the hairline. She took out her phone and shone a light in his ear. She snapped her fingers in irritation she was looking at the wrong side. This side was furthest from the window. She turned his head towards her and walked round to the other side of the drawer there was just enough room for her between the drawer and the wall. There was nothing in the ear, nothing under the hair on the neck. She stretched the skin on the neck smoothing out the wrinkles. Then she saw it, a tiny pinprick of a hole behind the ear right on the crease of the beginning of the lobe. She took a photograph of it.

"Sullivan."

She jumped and dropped her phone onto Simmons bare chest and turned to see Speed standing at the door.

"A touch of déjà vu what on earth are you doing here? You're not on the force as I understand it now," he said taking out his phone starting to dial.

"I know how Simmons died."

He froze still staring at his phone and looked up. "So do I... natural causes."

"It was well planned. You were on a list of suspects taking calls from Simmons in HQ. You arranged to meet him by the jetty, probably offering to give him some more information. You got out of your car and stood by his door ensuring that he couldn't open it so he had to wind the electric window down. You leaned forward pretending to whisper something in his ear and injected him with some deadly quick acting poison. He would have felt it of course and while he was trying to work out what had happened you put your hand inside centrally locking all the doors and press the window up button. It closed as Simmons was dying and you knew your job was done. His body would come to you in the morgue but even if it didn't, nobody could test for an obscure poison if they didn't know what it was. The perfect murder. You were undone by the weather. Had Simmons been found where you left him that would have been it. But the freak snap thaw made the car slowly slide down the pier into the river. Then it snowed and the temperature dropped again. The strange circumstances called for a more careful examination of the case revealing Simmons background. Harriet put her left hand to her head as more images flashed in her mind. It was definitely Speedy's face. She was swaying feeling a little dizzy and steadied herself by holding on to the edge of the drawer. She was aware that Speed was walking round the marble topped table in the middle of the room and with only a slight pause in his step opened a drawer from beneath the table and took something out. Her exit was now blocked between the drawer and the wall.

"You know Harriet I have worked with and for, many policemen and women over the years. Some have been good, some brilliant and some exceptional. But you Harriet are the best." He was getting nearer. "However you only have a theory, no evidence whatsoever and tomorrow, Simmons will be cremated. You have no authority here you are simply a member of the public and you have illegally entered police premises."

He was within four feet now. Harriet saw something glint in his right hand.

"Disappear into obscurity, go somewhere nice and enjoy your inheritance, relax and get a life.

Speed lunged forward and at the same time Harriet caught his wrist and twisted it. She saw he was holding a small syringe. He grabbed her throat with his left hand and pushed her head back against the wall, he was surprisingly strong. The needle in his right hand came closer to her face almost touching her cheek. Her gun was in her left pocket but she was holding his wrist with her left hand and pushing at his chest with her right. The artery in her neck was throbbing as her circulation was being cut off. She started to feel faint and knew she had to make a desperate attempt to get her gun. She let go and stuck a finger in his eye making him recoil for a split second allowing her to release the grip of his wrist with her left hand which went straight to her pocket and without aiming fired off four rounds in rapid succession burning holes in her jacket pockets. The bullets caught him by surprise, one in the groin two in the stomach and one in the chest. She caught his hand and saw the tip of the hypo still with a droplet of poison dangling from the one inch long sharp needle. His eyes closed and his knees buckled. She kept hold of his wrist as he slid down smearing her with blood and ended on his knees propped against her trapping her while still holding the needle. She stood dazed not believing what had just happened. She tried to clear her head, what to do, call in and report what had happened or leave. She picked up the phone from Simmons chest and dialled 911.

"I'd like to report a death."

"A death?, where are you Ma'am?"

"I'm in the morgue at Police HQ."

"Is this some kind of joke?"

"No I'm not being funny my name is Harriet Sullivan. I have just shot Dr Henry Speed in self-defence."

She had reasoned that they would have cremated Simmons destroying the evidence if she had gone into hiding. The door burst open and two uniforms officers with guns pointing shouted at Harriet to put the gun on the floor and kneel down. She closed the drawer and stepped side-way allowing Speed to fall forward against the wall, put the gun on the floor next to him and kneeled down. Then they put the cuffs on her helped her up and took her outside into the cells. "Be careful of the poison in the hypo," she said.

"Ms Sullivan my name is Sergeant Darrel and as I'm sure you I've taken over from Sergeant Stokes. You are under arrest for first degree murder, breaking and entering do you wish to make a statement?

"Do you know who I am?"

"Of course I do you're former Detective Sullivan."

"I didn't break in, I know the universal code. I had been working on a homicide where a man called Simmons was killed. If you analyse the poison in the hypo and test Simmons you'll find the same poison in his body. Speed killed him. He knew that he had been found out and attacked me with the syringe. I shot him in self-defence."

Darrel avoided her gaze and fiddled with his pen turning it round and round. "Found out, what do you mean? Why would Speed want to kill Simmons?"

"Because Simmons thought he had discovered a connection between contract killers, the Government, companies working for Defense and possibly even leading to some in the force like Speed."

"I've been fully briefed about you but I like to make up my own mind about people." He gave her a notebook and pen. "Make out a full report. If what you say pans out we'll drop the charges."

"I want my badge back."

Darrel whistled and shook his head. "And pigs can fly."

"I'll go to a tribunal for unfair dismissal. Who knows what evidence will be presented to the court. Could be embarrassing for some." She leaned forward. "Pass it on. Tell me something Sergeant who's side are you on?"

Darrel stood up glaring and leaned against the desk. "Ok this is how it's going to be. You're on medical leave for six months after which, pending an all-clear from the medic and all the other minor details like shooting medical examiners and breaking and entering, you will get your badge back. Whether you work for me or not is another matter."

Harriet looked up at the monitor mounted on the wall.

"Detective Harriet Sullivan can't keep out of the news. SLCPD have released this statement, 'Top medical examiner Dr Henry Speed has been killed in a shooting in his own morgue. Detective Sullivan was released without charge after claiming that she was in fear of her life and it was in self-defence. The police continue investigating the circumstances because of a possible link between Dr Speed and the death of Joseph Gideon Simmons whose body was found in his car recovered from the Jordan River."

"Can I borrow a tablet Ben?"

"What for?"

"I need it to plug in Brian's hard drive."

"No that won't work you can't plug the hard drive into a tablet. Here take this laptop. Listen you'd better skedaddle while you're ahead, even your luck will run out eventually. The new Sergeant is from the school of hard-liners, know what I mean, very ambitious."

"Ok I'll be in Jan's if you need me."

As Harriet left the Salt Lake City Public Safety Building she hadn't noticed that she was being watched. The Northerly wind blowing down 475 South, quickened her step. She was grateful to enter the warmth of the Diner, busy with office workers taking an early lunch break. Her usual table in the corner was occupied so she settled for one in the middle of a line along the window. Jan was very busy but managed to give her a wave. Harriet opened the laptop, turned it on and plugged in the hard drive.

"What would you like today Harriet?"

"Today's special Jan, thanks." She clicked on the external drive icon and up came pages of folders. "Wow Brian you have been a busy boy," she thought.

Jan left a mug of coffee and dashed off. The ambient sounds mostly of small time office politics got a little louder. Harriet clicked on a folder marked shipping. A thumbnail of jpegs appeared, images of scanned waybill documents, customs stamps notifications, barcode freight journey progress stages. This was undeniable evidence of illegal shipments of minerals entering the US disguised as fertilizer, nitrates and various agricultural chemicals. She clicked on a folder marked emails. Thousands perhaps hundreds of thousands appeared. Many were highlighted. She clicked on the first and nearly fell off her seat.

Hi Clive,
We in the Department are relieved and delighted that our countries industries are future proofed thanks to the work you and your company have done. It was a source of great concern to all here and in the Whitehouse. Keep up the good work.
Decker

"Close that computer and eat your lunch." Said Jan placing a dish of tempura shrimp and salad on the table.

Harriet moved it aside picked up a shrimp dipping it in the sauce and took a bite while clicking on another email. Her eyes grew wider. Email after email exposed the whole corrupt network of officials, company bosses and…police! Her heart missed a beat as her finger poised over an email. She was just about to press it.

"Harriet I've been looking for you."

It was a man's voice. She looked up and closed the laptop. He sat down opposite her with a beaming smile. "Do I know you?" she asked.

It was Briscoe. He winced, "know me? Its George…George Hanson how could you forget, I'm your boyfriend, well boyfriend is maybe a little strong since we only got to know each other maybe over a week or so. What a time we had though and then you disappeared."

"I...I've lost my memory, I'm sorry," she shook her head, "no...you must have the wrong person."

George Briscoe smiled. "No Harriet I have the right Harriet Constance Sullivan. I'm so pleased to see you. You're looking as gorgeous as ever."

"Everything Ok darlin'?" Jan asked putting a glass of water on the table.

"Yes...yes."

"What can I get you sir?"

Briscoe was typing a text on his phone. "I'm good," he said.

Harriet dipped another prawn into the sauce dip and chewed it. She shook her head. "Are you serious...look I have lost my memory but I can't believe I wouldn't remember having a... did we...?"

"...What sleep together? We certainly did. Well, maybe not so much of the sleeping."

"Do you have any ID?"

"No not with me. I'm afraid I was rather naughty. The police caught me driving after I'd had one or two drinks. They took my license away." He gestured, "I have nothing else here."

"Prove we slept together," she said eating another prawn.

"What?"

"Prove it to me."

Briscoe looked around the Diner. "What here?" he whispered.

"Yes."

"Ok, well…you have on your person a *Polyommatus coridon*."

"What's that?" she smiled.

"Your tattoo, it's a Chalk Hill Blue butterfly, very beautifully done and very tasteful placed on your hip just inside the left hipbone. You have faded bruises across most of your ribs from…I think you said falling out of a car? You have a small mole under your left breast and an old scar on your right knee. You have…"

"…Ok enough. Can it be true?" Harriet put her hand to her mouth and stared at him. How could she forget someone she slept with? Was that even possible?

"Look I'm sorry it must have come as a shock. Tell you what I've ordered an uber cab, why don't we go back to my place I have ID there and we can get to know each other all over again and that'll be a lot of fun."

"I…I have work to do."

"Here in a Diner? You can work at my place. It's much more comfortable." He leaned forward and kissed her on the lips taking her by surprise.

The office workers had paid and were leaving. Jan was very uncomfortable with the attention Harriet was receiving and her mouth opened as the stranger kissed Harriet.

"Let me get this," he said picking up the check. He walked over to the till and handed Jan $30 and the check.

"Do I know you?"

"No," he said walking back to the table, "there's the cab waiting."

Harriet stood up put on her coat and picked up the laptop. She smiled at George and followed him out. Jan watched them get into the back seat of the car. She took a note of the number and as Gleb Durchenko reversed and drove off she picked up the phone.

27

The Washington Post newsroom was quiet apart from mouse and keyboards clicking. Several monitors hung from the ceiling showing a satellite news channel with the sound off. Next to the open newsroom in a large hall at the top of a set of stairs was a large table seating six journalists in an editorial meeting planning the following days' paper. Newspapers covered the table along with notepads and tablets.

News Editor Steven Jessel threw down the Salt Lake City Tribune and smiled. "Not a bad paper that."

"Parochial," said Karina Holsen, Chief reporter.

"Of course it's parochial though I prefer to use the word local, that's its job and it does it really well. However it doesn't have any more detail about the Sullivan story. Karina how is that shaping?"

"Ok let's start with what we know and then we can move onto speculation. Detective Sullivan was working on a series of related deaths purporting to be either accidental or suicide, let's just call them sudden deaths. These enquiries had already been closed. She had found something linking all these deaths meaning they were murdered."

"What was the link?"

"Well we don't even know who the victims were. Let's stick to what we know. The FBI caught practically an army of hired killers and my contact has told me that the tip off came from…"

She spread her arms in question mode.

"...Harriet Sullivan?"

"Yup. So this is one helluva smart cookie that could have taken all the credit and didn't want it. Now what the hell were all these contractors doing in America, who for and how did they slip into the country so easily. Well I think and let's not get ahead of ourselves here, that they were the ones responsible for the string of killings. What does Sullivan do then? Bearing in mind she has already survived two attempts to kill her according to my sources, she goes to Brazil. The FBI and the DEA claim she is there to meet with a major drug dealer. She is arrested coming back into the country and disappears probably spirited off to some unlisted black site. Then she is released. The FBI drop all charges and claim she has had a nervous breakdown, wouldn't you have a nervous breakdown if you were treated like that? As a result she can't remember anything very much about the case. Convenient don't you think? The top Medical Examiner in Salt Lake City Dr Henry Speed is shot in his own morgue by?"

"Harriet Sullivan."

"Correct. He had in his possession, in his right hand to be exact a hypo with a deadly poison that they are still analysing to find out what the heck it is but what they have established is that further tests on Joseph Simmons body, do you remember him? He was a freelance investigative journalist found dead in very strange circumstances. The tests proved he was killed with the same poison that Speed was trying to kill Sullivan with when she shot him. Just to make things more complicated Sullivan's ex; Mitch was digging into this story and ended up critically ill in hospital. That's what we know." She gestured for comment.

"Is she back to work?"

"Medical leave, six months.

"So who's taken over the case?"

Karina shrugged, "there's absolutely nothing coming out of the SLCPD except that there are new faces in homicide and old ones moved out."

"There's a helluva lot missing from this story. Karina see if you can get a statement from the Governor of Utah...what's his name?"

"Samuel Hooker."

"These victims, if we knew who they were we could find the link. Find the link and we find the motive. We need to speak to Harriet Sullivan. Karina find her."

Ben was in a panic. "Jeff where are you?"

"Just packing up some things."

"Thank God you're still in town. I just got a call from Jan, you know, at the diner, Harriet's left with two men. Have you still got the department mobile?"

"Yes."

Ok I'll patch in the GPS link from her laptop."

"Laptop?"

"Yes she's got one of my laptops, and the Utah plate number is ALZ 364, good luck."

Briscoe was holding Harriet's right hand and while it seemed a bit strange to her it was also comforting.

"Where do you live?" she asked.

"On the north edge of town, we're not far."

The streets and houses were giving way to fields and lanes.

They were approaching a low building that had a sign saying 'Northern City Livestock Mart'.

Harriet looked at Briscoe with the first pang of fear and pulled her hand away. "Is this it?"

He ignored her. They stopped next to a maze of pens and corrals full of sheep and cattle. Briscoe leaned across and opened Harriet's door and slid over keeping a hold of her arm, pushing her. She had the laptop in her left hand and slipped it under the vehicle as she got out.

"You're not my boyfriend are you?"

"Harriet given any other circumstances I would love to be your boyfriend alas you're right, I'm not. Inside."

"Can I help you folks?"

A caretaker stood at the entrance to the mart. Durchenko shot him in the head and he fell to the ground. They stepped over the body and stood at the entrance to a medium sized amphitheatre with tiers of stone seats descending to the show ring.

"You're animals." Briscoe gave her a push. "How did you know about my tattoo?"

"You were naked on the trolley when we tricked you into giving the information we were looking for."

"We?"

"Dr Speed and I."

"He's dead."

"I know. Think nothing of it we weren't friends just business colleagues."

"This is not necessary, I still don't remember anything."

"We couldn't take the risk. There was always the possibility that you would get your memory back."

"Lots of people will be looking for me."

"Oh didn't you know? You've gone on holiday to recover from all your adventures, Bermuda I believe. At least that's what your friends will think."

"Oh? And how will they get that impression?"

"You emailed them, through an intermediary of course."

"Get on with it," said Gleb impatiently.

"They'll find me," she said.

"Not in a million years. There's a deep pit probably an old mine shaft where rotten carcases are disposed of and then covered with quicklime. Come on I'll show you, through that door."

They left the rear of the building and walked towards a roped off area. Gleb fell to the ground as the sound of a shot rang out. Briscoe ran for cover and Harriet dived into a large corral of young cattle. Two more shots were fired puncturing the tyres with an audible hiss. Briscoe was inside the mart and stopped at the entrance scanning the horizon. It was only a short distance, a matter of fifteen yards to the car and even with two flats it would still get him far enough away from the shooter. Jeff looked down on the scene. He could see where Harriet was and as long as she stayed there, she would be safe. He changed the setting of the SG 551 assault rifle mark 1 single to 20, automatic and aimed at the gas tank.

"You aint going anywhere Briscoe."

Briscoe sprinted towards the car just as Jeff opened up raking the vehicle with bullets. One hit the tank and the car exploded killing Briscoe. Crazed cattle broke through fences and ran off in a cloud of dust. One caught Harriet throwing her against a wall. Jeff scampered slipping and sliding down the hill and found

Harriet unconscious with a graze on the side of her head. He checked for a mobile signal but there was none. He picked her up and carried her back to where his car was parked. He sat her in the passenger seat and checked his phone again. There was an intermittent signal. He dialled 911 and was cut off.

"Damn," he said. Harriet groaned and moved her head. "Harriet are you alright." She opened her eyes. He tried calling again and got through. "Blackwell there's been a shooting...The Northern City Livestock Marts...Ok."

"What happened?" she asked.

"You were hit by a steer."

"The laptop."

"Where is it?"

"Under the car."

Jeff ran down the hill to the still burning car. He broke off a piece of fence post and fished the hot laptop out. He carried it up the hill on his forearms protected by his jacket sleeves until he reached the vehicle. "It looks Ok, I'm sure the hard drive is alright if nothing else works. They're pretty tough," he looked at her. "What on earth possessed you to go off with Briscoe?"

"You know him?"

"Sure. He's one, was one of the rogue FBI agents. I don't know who the other guy was I didn't get a chance to ask him."

Harriet started laughing as the sirens in the distance got louder surprising Jeff.

"He said he was my boyfriend."

"You can thank your surrogate mother, Jan. If she hadn't acted quickly phoning Ben, well who knows. Look, this can't go on. You've got to do something to get your memory back."

28

"Reports are coming in of a shooting at the Northern City Livestock Marts. Two men are said to have died at the scene near a burned out vehicle. SLCPD say they are not looking for anyone in connection with the incident."

Darrel switched off the sound and turned round.

"Let me get this straight. Briscoe convinced you that he was your boyfriend to get you out of the Diner and took you to a quiet spot to kill you. The owner of the Diner was suspicious and called IT? I'm trying very hard to understand all of this. Why would she call Ben in IT?"

"She knows him, he eats there regularly."

"So far so good. Ben calls you Jeff, how did you follow the car?"

"Ben gave me a GPS locater link on the laptop Harriet had."

"Alright you two I want a full report on my desk within the hour."

"I don't work here anymore, remember."

"Don't get smart with me Sullivan. Have you had that wound checked out?"

"I'm alright."

Darrel shrugged and looked at Blackwell. "Shouldn't you be in Ogden?"

"I have some leave left and we're still house hunting."

"Is there something going on I should know about?" They shook their heads. "George Briscoe, a loose cannon sacked by the FBI without comment, dead. The other guy, Gleb Durchenko the contractor gangmaster, dead, Henry Speed dead. Everywhere you go Sullivan you leave a trail of dead bodies behind you. Get out of here and write that report."

Sullivan left the office and went to her desk which was occupied. "Beat it buddy I've got a report to write for the Sergeant. Its Ok you can have it when I've finished." Harriet sat down just as her phone rang. "Sullivan...who?...Ok I'll come to reception."

Sullivan swung open the door and looked at the desk Sergeant. He nodded at a young woman sitting at a coffee table reading a magazine from the rack. "Alison Simmons?"

"Yes are you Detective Sullivan?"

Harriet nodded. "I didn't know Mr and Mrs Simmons had a daughter. Would you like a tea or coffee?"

"No thanks. I'm afraid I didn't get on with Dad. I still heard from Mum from time to time but as the years went by, less and less. I live in San Francisco now and I'm here to settle my parents estate, you know meet with lawyers and banks but I also came to see you. I'm relieved that you found out what really happened to them but I know very little."

"Would you mind showing me some ID? Sometimes journalists get up to all kinds of tricks to get information."

"Of course." Alison looked in her bag and found her driving license.

"Thanks. Your father died of a rare, difficult to detect, poison. He was in his car when Henry Speed injected him with it. He died instantly. The doors were locked and his window wound up and that would have been that except for a freak sudden change in the weather. After Speed left, the car slid down the slipway into the water. That led to a more rigorous investigation. Speed is dead. Your mother was shot and they made it look like suicide, why I don't know. I'm not sure exactly who did it but I do know the killer is either dead or in prison. Your father was a very brave man, he found out about the illegal activity of two large companies which led to his death. Your mother was in the wrong place at the wrong time. I'm very sorry."

"Another two dead what's the official line?" Steven Jessel was stirring his coffee.

"Cops are not looking for anyone else but there's precious little detail however my contact says that Sullivan is connected."

"Who is this woman? Can we get hold of her Karina?"

"She's at Police HQ."

"Get our local correspondent to stake out the building and stay there until she comes out. This story just keeps running and running but where to, that's the question?"

Jeff knocked on Darrel's door and entered putting both reports on his desk. He ignored Jeff and continued working on the computer.

"Come on let's get out of here he said to Harriet."

Unfamiliar faces gazed at them from various desks as they made their way out.

"Have you still got the laptop?"

"It's in the car."

"Where are we going?"

"To see a friend of mine."

"But we need to check out what's on the laptop."

"This can't wait." He swung open the outside door and let her out first.

"Excuse me Detective Sullivan I'm Morrison from the Washington Post I wonder if we could talk?" They kept walking. "It's about the serial killings."

Harriet stopped. "What?"

"We got the piece from Mitch before he was attacked."

"I'm sorry I can't discuss that with you."

"What's the link?"

"Excuse me?"

"We don't even know the names of the dead how were they connected?"

Harriet looked at Jeff who said, "I'm sorry right at this moment we can't give any comment. Who's your news editor?"

"Steven Jessel."

"Ok we'll bear that in mind."

The windows were shuttered and the walls painted a pastel green were bare. On top of a hard wearing grey tile carpet was a square mustard coloured rug with a small wooden coffee table and a simple lamp supporting a grey shade next to a comfortable grey leather armchair. Adjacent to it was a black leather adjustable couch lit by a standard lamp under a black shade. The two lamps were the only illumination in the room, minimal fuss, minimal distraction.

"Just to be clear," said Doctor Reece opening a brown folder. "I am not a consultant I don't usually take on individual cases. I moved on from that when I began teaching, however when Detective Blackwell contacted me, I was sceptical and then I remembered that Peter your family Doctor is an old friend of mine. Added to that of course the publicity that has been generated speculating about your adventures is intriguing. I've had your report from the Hospital and you may have suffered damage to certain parts of the brain due to the effects of a drug that lowers acetylcholine levels affecting memory. I have to warn you that hypnosis is not like any other field of medicine, it doesn't always work. I never make promises but I do enjoy a challenge and you are to say the least, somewhat of a challenge. Does that all make sense?" Harriet nodded. "Has anyone tried to hypnotize you before?"

"Yes. Peter had a go. I suffered from claustrophobia."

"And did it help."

"No. He said I was a subject that couldn't be hypnotized."

"What happened?"

"My father took me potholing and that cured it, or at least I learned how to control it."

"Well that must have been some time ago, techniques have moved on since the swinging pocket watch days. For those most resistant to hypnotherapy we use a low dose of nitrous oxide."

"Laughing gas?"

He nodded. "Yes that's what its commonly known as. It improves suggestibility by 36%. However we only need a dose that will relax not send you into hysterics. Amongst some people there is a conscious resistance. Some might describe them as control freaks and this drug simply allows a peaceful contentment. You will be awake at all times, you will not be under my spell and you will not do anything you don't want to do, Ok?"

She nodded. He gave her an inhaler with the gas.

"Now take a deep breath and hold it for ten seconds. Now exhale slowly. Your eyelids will begin to feel heavy. I want you to concentrate on your breathing, focus on breathing in and out, in and out. Your eyelids are closing. I want you to imagine that you are at the top of a staircase with ten steps. Each step is deeper into your subconscious. Step nine; relax the muscles in your feet and legs. You are feeling drowsy. Your eyes are closing. Step eight; relax the muscles in your arms starting from the fingers, the wrist and the forearm. Step seven; keep focussing on your breathing, in and out. Step six; you are entering a subconscious state. Step five, relax the shoulder muscles. Step four; allow your head to drop forward onto your chest. Step three; you have reached a deep subconscious state." He paused glancing at his watch. "Can you hear me Harriet?" he said gently.

"Yes."

"Good I'm going to cast your mind back to the morning of the first of January 2017...where are you?"

"It's cold. I'm at a slipway next to Jordan River. There's a car being pulled out. It has a dead body inside his name is Jo Simmons married to Melissa, she's dead too."

"Tell me about Brazil."

"There's a police helicopter firing at us. The driver and his passenger are dead."

"Ok let's go forward in time, you're back in Utah what happened?"

"Arrested by the FBI, they're taking me to a black site. I'm on my own. I'm floating in a tank, no light, no sound, nothing. Ugh I'm cold again; naked on a slab of marble in the morgue. Speed is going to perform an autopsy on me. I can hear the saw." Tears began coursing down her cheeks. "I can't move. He has cut off my legs and arms, I just want to die...I'm in hospital, I'm Ok, I don't understand."

"Harriet you are safe. I am going to count backwards from five and you will come out of the trance. You will remember everything you have said and done since your memory loss. Five, four, three, two, one." He snapped his fingers.

Harriet opened her eyes in wonder and brushed away the tears. "My God. You're a genius. I remember everything now, everything."

29

The five star Lapin restaurant was busy. On the wooden balcony Clive Bailey lifted his glass and gazed at the clarity of the Domaine Leflaive Batard Montrachet with its aromas of pear, smoky butterscotch orange peel, honey and vanilla. This was by far his favourite white wine. He sipped and closed his eyes for a moment then looked across the table at Jennifer, his wife.

"Isn't that heaven?"

She looked away. He always overplayed his knowledge of wines.

"We haven't heard from Maurice for a while, is everything Ok?"

"Look at that sky."

Horizontal intermingling tendrils of cloud tinged with gold that would soon be red put on a display against the early evening sky.

"Of course everything's Ok. There's always going to be a bit of rough and tumble that's what business is all about. Why do you ask?"

"I haven't seen him smile for a very long time."

"Did you know Red's not well?" Clive looked at Jennifer. "He's only got a few months to live. He may be the lucky one."

"What do you mean?" she said. Clive didn't answer. "I can't say I'm surprised considering the lifestyle he led I feel sorry for his poor wife."

"They'll all be fine."

A well-dressed young woman with a shoulder bag looked around the restaurant and saw the Bailey's on the balcony. She approached.

"Excuse me Mrs Bailey." She whispered something in his ear.

"Ok Dorothy, business Mrs B, I'll just be a couple of minutes." They found a quiet spot at the corner of the bar. "Tell me again."

"There's been a breach of one of our servers. It's a worm. We're analysing it but it looks like an off the shelf buy it on the internet type...untraceable. What we don't know is how it got there. The possibilities are an online hacker...very unlikely with the best state of the art anti-virus architecture money can buy. Or it was somebody in-house. I think that's the most likely. We've been checking staff access and we are narrowing it down."

"Ok exactly what have they accessed."

Dorothy licked her lips "They managed to get into the encrypted folders."

Clive Bailey's face went white. He clutched at the bar to steady himself. "Could it be a shake-down, ransomware?"

"There's been nothing, its deathly quiet."

"Get the whole IT department on it we have to find out who it is." Clive returned to his table and Jennifer.

"You look terrible, what's happened."

"Just a hiccup." He sat down and took out his phone texting his brother Maurice.

'Get into the office there has been a serious breach of a server.'

"What do we do with all this hacked material?" asked Jeff.

"Not what do we do but who do we trust."

"That's easy, nobody."

"That's cool so what's left."

"I don't know, Harriet stop playing games."

"Sorry Jeff. Let's look at the options. Our only issue is Brian. What he's given us is dynamite but he needs protection."

"Why don't we select the most important emails and files without releasing everything? Surely Brian would be Ok."

"Ok so we go through the material looking for specific phrases or words and put all the relevant stuff into one folder."

"Well we could use a throwaway email address collected through a VPN. Then what? Who do we send it to?"

"Who else? The President of the United States of America, Alvera Yolanda. I don't need an anonymous email address, I'll use my own."

"You're taking a huge risk. She may know all about it. Do you want to spend the rest of your days in Guantanamo."

"I've always wanted to see Cuba."

"Seriously."

"I have to take that risk. Look an email out of the blue with such damning information needs provenance. Don't you think the US Government is good at faking such things? Of course they are. I'm putting myself out there to get attention and authenticate the material."

Jeff shook his head. "You're crazy. Look will you promise me one thing? When this is all over resign. Leave the force, enjoy your inheritance, think about it?"

"Now you're the one that's crazy. I'm going home. I feel safe now that all the bad guys are dead or in jail."

"Maybe not all of them."

Harriet was expecting carnage when she opened the door. Bullet holes in the walls, blood on the floor, smashed furniture but the walls were repaired and painted, damaged furniture was replaced and the floor had been cleaned.

"Thank You Sarge," she said.

It felt different being at home again in a nice way. She powered up the computer and plugged in Brian's hard drive. It didn't take long to find all the incriminating emails shipping documents, links from Cutler and the Baileys to their contacts. The extent of the network was laid bare for all to see. FBI special agent George Briscoe, Decker Stadler Secretary of Defense, Under Secretary of Defense for Acquisitions Arnie Brinkman, Utah Police Deputy Chief Bingham, Utah Assistant District Attorney Bradley Hooper and Utah's Medical Examiner Dr Henry Speed were all implicated. She checked online for a contact email address for the president and of course it was president@whitehouse.gov.

'Dear Madam President
I and my colleagues have discovered a network of corruption surrounding the illegal importation of Niobium. Two companies sought to corner the market in this rare earth mineral by forcibly acquiring foreign mining companies that resulted in many innocent deaths. They employed imported contractors to murder whistle blowers and threaten the families of some employees who they needed to continue working. The material in the attached folder is entirely authentic. I am willing to vouch for the accuracy and reliability of the source whose life is now in danger. The reason I am sending you this, is because I am still not entirely sure who to trust.
Yours sincerely
Harriet Sullivan,
Homicide Detective Salt Lake City Police Department.'

Harriet attached the folder, closed her eyes, took a deep breath and pressed send. She suddenly felt really tired, showered put on her pyjamas and immediately fell asleep.

The doorbell rang. Harriet opened her eyes still half asleep. She dragged herself out of bed as the bell rang again and opened the curtains. There was a man in a suit with an earpiece leaning against a black car. She put on a dressing gown and went downstairs. "Who is it?"

Ms Sullivan we've been sent by the President, she wants to meet you."

Harriet opened the door and put her hand out. "Can I see your ID please."

"We're Secret Service agents from the President's personal security team."

Harriet studied the badge. "Come in."

"No Ma'am we'll wait for you outside."

Harriet closed the door ran upstairs, took a very quick shower, took longer to choose a dress and left, closing and locking her door. They smiled and opened the rear door for her. Before long she was being driven through the VIP gate at the airport where a small civilian jet was waiting. The engines were turning as she went up the small stairs and stepped inside while the door closed behind her. It was small but a lot quieter than she expected. A steward appeared with breakfast when the jet levelled at a cruising height of 39,000 ft. Just under four hours later it was touching down at Washington Dulles International where the Presidential Marine One helicopter, a green Sikorsky S-92, was waiting.

"Sir, we've got him."

Clive Bailey looked up from the computer monitor on his desk. "Who is it?"

"Brian Irving in IT. I've cut off access from his terminal to the servers."

"Get security to bring him up here." He picked up the phone. "Maurice we found the hacker."

"Who is it?"

"Some nobody in IT"

"How did he do it?"

"I don't know yet..." The door opened and in walked Brian flanked by two security guards. "...I'll call you back." He stared at Brian for a few seconds then stood up slowly and walked round his desk. "I'll call you when I need you." He said dismissing the guards. "What is it Brian? Do we not pay you enough? Is the work too boring or too difficult. Were you planning to sell the information to a competitor...mm? I know what you stole but I'd like to hear it from you." Brian kept his head down looking at his shoes and stayed silent. "What did you do with the files folders and emails you stole?" he said emphasizing the last word by banging on his desk making Brian jump. "I'm hoping there is still time to limit the damage you have done to this company but I need to know some things from you."

"I don't care what you do, it won't make any difference."

"So you don't care about yourself. Who do you care about?"

Brian's eyes widened. "Leave my mother out of this."

"You shouldn't have taken what does not belong to you. I'm not playing games."

"I gave it all to the police. It's over Mr Bailey all over."

"Which cop?"

"Detective Sullivan."

The door opened and several uniformed officers came in. "Mr Clive Bailey?"

"Yes."

"Turn round please, sir." Hands were pushed behind his back and handcuffs fastened both wrists. "You are under arrest. There are numerous charges which will be brought before you when we are ready. Your brother Maurice has also been arrested."

Red Cutler was watering Hyacinths in his conservatory when his wife came in followed by four uniformed policemen.

30

Harriet was shown into the oval office. It was bigger than she expected. She stood in front of the imposing Carrera marble fireplace flanked by ionic columns and looked up at the portrait of George Washington. To the left of a flush partially hidden door on the wall was Abe Lincoln. She wondered what they would have done. She turned and stood at the end of one of the two sofas and examined the Resolute desk, a gift from Queen Victoria made from oak from the expeditionary ship the Resolute. A glass panelled door opened and in came President Yolanda carrying a brief case followed by aides. She came striding forward and stuck out her hand

"Detective Sullivan can I call you Harriet?"

Yes, of course Madam President."

"Alvera, please have a seat I've ordered some tea and coffee."

The President put the briefcase on the floor next to the coffee table and sat down opposite Harriet. She opened the case and took out some notes putting on a pair of glasses.

"It says here that you have been kidnapped twice and three attempts have been made on your life."

"Four, it's four times actually."

"This country owes you a debt of gratitude that would be impossible to repay. I have already acted on the information you have given us, Robert, if you please?"

"Yes ma'am," said the aide referring to his tablet. "Decker Stadler Secretary of Defense has resigned pending investigation by the FBI. The Attorney General has a copy of the files and it's up to him to decide whether there will be any charges. At the moment there is no evidential link between the imported contract killers and Bailey and Bailey or for that matter Universal Defence and Development Contractors Corporation. Under Secretary of Defense for Acquisitions Arnie Brinkman has been arrested so has Deputy Chief Bingham and Bradley Hooper."

"Thank you Robert." A tray of coffee tea and biscuits arrived and left on the coffee table. "There will no doubt be many other arrests as this sorry business unravels. Tea or coffee?"

"Tea please."

She began pouring out the tea. "Harriet the only part of all of this I agreed to was to ensure that America had a long term dependable supply of rare earth minerals but not at any cost. The tactics used by the Baileys and Cutler, corrupting officials faking import permits using murderers to do their dirty work was totally unacceptable. Those who thought it was a price worth paying for will be dealt with, no matter what the political fallout. You continued your investigation despite all the dangers, the attempts on your life, the death of your uncle. Others would have given up. Of course we have little influence in the affairs of the State of Utah and it would be entirely at the discretion of the Utah Governor but I'm sure that when the full story is known there will undoubtedly be promotion."

Harriet smiled and shook her head. "Alvera I would prefer to remain a Detective in Homicide a desk job is not for me but right now I would be happy just to get my job back, I'm on six months medical leave. Would it be possible for Detective Blackwell and Sergeant Stokes to be reinstated in the department?"

Alvera Yolanda grinned and winked. "Make a note of that

Robert."

"The Washington Post have bits of the story. My ex-boyfriend was working for them. He was following up the story about all the sudden deaths and ended up in hospital. He's still on the critical list. It's not for me to be releasing statements to the press is your Press office planning a statement? I ask that because I'd like the Post to have a head start but it's not my call."

"What do you think Robert?"

"I'm sure the Press Secretary can work something out."

Washington Post News Editor Steven Jessel burst into Arnault Jollenbeck's office breathing heavily. "You're not going to believe this Arnie we've just got the scoop of the century. This is a press release from the Oval Office and it has a tag saying exclusive courtesy of Harriet Sullivan. It's all here. Resignations in the Defense Department, a whole lot of senior officials arrested. Police officers in Utah, serial killings linked to two big Corporations...this is huge."

"That Sullivan is quite a lady, Steven send her a big bouquet of flowers with a note."

Harriet had a text summoning her. She walked into Police HQ reception. The desk sergeant, detectives, office staff and uniformed officers stopped what they were doing and spontaneously applauded, cheered and whistled much to her surprise and embarrassment. She waved, climbed the stairs and swung open the door to Homicide. Everyone stood and applauded her. Her desk was empty apart for a bouquet of flowers. Jeff was standing next to his grinning from ear to ear and gave her a hug. Sergeant Stokes came out of his office applauding and gave her the most awkwardness of hugs. He stood back and looked at her shaking his head as the applauding died down.

"You wrote to the President of the United States of America. Haven't I told you enough times…everything goes through me?"

There was laughter and cries of speech, speech.

Harriet put her hands up. "The real hero was a small guy, an IT techie who lost his twin brother to a hired killer. He was just another regular Joe who had the guts to search for the evidence at great risk to himself. He fought fear with courage and gave the files to me. Without him there would have been no justice, no accountability no freedom from tyranny brought about by corporate greed. His name is Brian Irving, he's the hero."

Stokes took Harriet by the arm into his office. "Here." He opened a drawer took a badge and a gun and put it on the desk. "That's yours the holiday's over. There's a file on your desk and a body in the morgue. It's a sudden death, check it out."

She smiled and picked up the badge She was just about to leave and turned.

"Oh whose the new Medical Examiner."

"Don't you know?" asked Grainger. Harriet shook her head. "His name is Speed."

"What?"

"Dr Jason Speed, Henry's son."

"I didn't know he had a son. Isn't that going to be a tad awkward seeing as I killed his father an' all?"

"You're just going to have to work something out. He's not like his father. Nobody chooses their parents just don't call him Speedy."

Harriet walked back to her desk, smelled the flowers and opened a small envelope containing a card.

From Arnault Jollenbeck Editor and all at the Washington Post paraphrasing Louis Farrakhan...

'Fear cannot end without justice,
there can be no justice without truth,
the truth cannot be heard without,
the fearlessness of youth.'

End

Printed in Great Britain
by Amazon

26139559R00136